CONFEDERATE NATION

CONFEDERATE NATION

*Special Appearance
by Elvis Presley*

A novel by

Michael Loyd Gray

iUniverse, Inc.
New York Lincoln Shanghai

CONFEDERATE NATION
Special Appearance
by Elvis Presley

Copyright © 2005 by No copyright

All rights reserved. No part of this book may be used or reproduced by any means, graphic, electronic, or mechanical, including photocopying, recording, taping or by any information storage retrieval system without the written permission of the publisher except in the case of brief quotations embodied in critical articles and reviews.

iUniverse books may be ordered through booksellers or by contacting:

iUniverse
2021 Pine Lake Road, Suite 100
Lincoln, NE 68512
www.iuniverse.com
1-800-Authors (1-800-288-4677)

ISBN-13: 978-0-595-36516-6 (pbk)
ISBN-13: 978-0-595-67385-8 (cloth)
ISBN-13: 978-0-595-80950-9 (ebk)
ISBN-10: 0-595-36516-7 (pbk)
ISBN-10: 0-595-67385-6 (cloth)
ISBN-10: 0-595-80950-2 (ebk)

Printed in the United States of America

For Dorothy Gray, my mother, who understands.

From the Western Michigan University days I'd like to thank John Smolens, Stuart Dybek, Jil Larson, and John Cooley.

From the University of Illinois days my thanks goes to Daniel Curley, Joan Larsen Klein, and Rocco Fumento.

Special thanks to Joe Taylor in Grand Rapids, Michigan, who read my stuff and gave good advice.

Prologue

▼

July, 1864

Littlefield Hudson was a lanky 19-year-old from Virginia who had been made an officer because so many had been killed. Hardly a man was left from the regiment when it had mustered two years before, and now boys who showed any sense at all were made lieutenants. Hudson had showed some sense by not getting killed in May at Spotsylvania, and along the way the Confederate army had also discovered he knew which end of a horse the grain went in and which end it came out, and so it also made him a scout.

Not that there was enough grain to keep the horse's ribs from showing, or enough hardtack and beans to do the same for Hudson; but the lean, hungry look he shared with his horse, augmented by a straw hat and civilian clothes, was now helpful as he rode out of Frederick, Maryland, looking like a poor farmer instead of a Confederate scout for Gen. Jubal Early's Army of the Valley.

Forty-seven days had come and gone without rain. It was one of the hottest summers in memory, temperatures routinely over 90. It was already hot even though the sun was barely up as Hudson rode southeast of Frederick along the dusty Georgetown Pike until it crossed the Baltimore & Ohio Railroad tracks and then the lazy Monocacy River. Hudson watered his horse in the dark water, his eyes roaming over a green cornfield, looking for movement but it was still just corn and he moved on. He paused on the east bank to look back at a rail fence across the corn: men in white linen shirts and even a few women sheltering under parasols, were already sitting on it, waiting for the inevitable battle as Early's troops filed cautiously out of Frederick toward the river. Union forces were converging on the river from Baltimore. Hudson forded the river a mile south of a wooden bridge, a spot that later that day would provide the same service to Confederate cavalry under John McCausland.

From a rise, Hudson's experienced eyes scanned the fields, bridges, and roads, and it became very clear to him how it would play out. In his head, men and horses were already screaming. The muddy, slippery banks of the river would trap soldiers long enough for their enemies to kill them, the bodies pitching heavily into the water, staining it red. Turtles would later gnaw on them as they bobbed in the slow current. Corpses would quickly litter the fields and swell grotesquely in the heat, hideous gases escaping with obscene sounds. The wounded would cry for water and then for their mothers. The curious townspeople along the fence would be in rifle range, but the fools among them would discover that too late. Well, it was their problem, Hudson told his horse as he spurred it along the river. He looked over his shoulder one last time for a glimpse of the army, but the roads from Frederick had disappeared under yellow-gray clouds of dust.

The river was full of bends. A heron flew lazily down it, skimming close to the water, and its long, tapered bill struck Hudson as funny. He laughed, but the laugh sounded too loud and echoed among the trees. He looked quickly over his shoulder, but nothing was there. He rode quietly along the bank and saw deer ahead drinking water. He stopped his horse to watch them, not wanting to disturb them for a moment. He felt they were entitled to have their drink. Then it came, the sound like a thunderclap, and the two deer bolted as Hudson cocked his head to the direction of the artillery fire. There were more thunderclaps, in quick succession, and Hudson wondered how the good citizens of Frederick, perched gaily on their fence, liked war now.

Just north of Greenfield Mills he saw a rider coming the opposite way, on the far bank, and he instinctively reached for the heavy Navy Colt tucked into his belt. He steered the horse behind a tree. It was a just a shirtless, scrawny boy, not so much younger than Hudson, no doubt captivated by the sound of cannon. Hudson didn't want to have to shoot him. It would be like shooting himself, in a way; but he might have to do it. Fortunately, the boy did not see him. Yes, yes, Hudson thought as the boy urged his horse to a gallop, that's one of the first things they teach you, boy—ride to the sound of the guns.

Hudson gladly rode away from the sound of the guns, detouring around the town and toward Sugar Loaf Mountain a spell before cutting back and picking up the river. The distant gunfire reminded him of his purpose and he spurred the horse to an easy canter for a while. Once they were past Greenfield Mills he reined in his horse and patted its neck affectionately. Much would be expected of them and they had to rest when they could. He saw no other riders and could no longer hear the cannon. He was headed south, toward the Potomac, and a part of him wondered what would happen if he just kept riding west until he reached California.

After a while the seven limestone arches of the Monocacy Aqueduct came into view, and then the mouth of the Monocacy emptying into the Potomac. Hudson dismounted and gazed across the river: Virginia. Home. It didn't look any different than Maryland, but just knowing it was home made it seem different, better. Still, he knew it was an illusion. Yankees were thicker in Virginia now than in Maryland. Hudson wished he could just quit the war and go home. But it wasn't that simple. He wished it was. Home had been reduced from a place to a state of mind with a delicate balance. It was no longer possible to get home by crossing a river. He had accepted for some time that he was part of something that had to play itself out. There would be no going home until it was all over—or he was dead.

His mission was to scout the approaches to Washington in case it actually became possible for Early to capture the city. Hudson had chosen the river route instead of the Washington Pike because the pike below Frederick belonged to the Yankees—and because, perhaps, the river would take him tantalizingly close to Virginia. He did not believe Early could attack the city. It was enough, really, for the army to just be in Frederick, where it surely had accomplished its mission of drawing troops from Grant's forces besieging Petersburg, deep in Virginia. Hudson expected that this dangerous foray into Maryland was practically over and Early would soon slip back into northern Virginia.

Hudson rode a ways along the Potomac until he saw a small dust cloud ahead. A Union patrol, no doubt, on a road to the river. Cavalry. He turned away and crossed a field into heavy woods. There was a road splitting the woods and a wooded rise. He watched the road a long time, until dusk, and then he rode across the road and mounted the rise. From it he saw a fort to the east—Ft. Reno, he guessed, and he knew he was likely west of Tenleytown and not so far from Georgetown. The city was stretched out just a few miles away, and to the southeast he saw something he couldn't quite make out: the unfinished dome of the capitol.

It was dark now, and he stood on the rise and peered through field glasses at the soft glow of the city. In 1861 the Confederates had a view toward the city from east of Manassas, across the Potomac, before that fleeting opportunity melted away and the war settled into bloody attrition. Washington was there for the taking. Could it be taken? Hudson didn't know. Probably not. He wondered if Early was even still coming. Maybe he had been beaten back on the Monocacy and even now was slithering back into Virginia. Without Hudson. He felt naked sitting practically on Washington's doorstep without the safety of the army. Would they come? Capturing Washington would surely mean an armistice. Everyone knew the North was tired of the war—Mr. Lincoln's war—and if it were an honorable armistice for the Confederacy, fine. But the war, Hudson felt, must end. Now. Whatever glory was to be found in war had faded years ago, and he had finally come to see it as murder by ideas.

Slavery was one of the murderous ideas. States rights was another. Hudson was from a modest town near Chesapeake Bay and didn't own slaves, didn't think he could ever own another human being; but he went along, blindly, stupidly, because men who were said to be great thinkers—Lee, Davis, and others—made it seem like God approved of the Southern Way and even demanded it. No, he didn't think much of slavery, but someone had said the black man wasn't ready for independence, that slavery was a necessary stage before negroes could be free. Hudson had finally realized that great idea smelled fishy, too.

It was the notion of states ruling themselves that had initially caught his fancy. There was even a Confederate general whose name was actually States Rights—States Rights Gist, a brigadier serving somewhere in the west. But what the hell was the concept of states rights once it had been examined? It was nothing more than selfishness, really—a sort of isolationism, and after all the killing he had seen and done, Hudson decided that leaving the union wasn't a great idea, nor was God behind it.

He looked up at the night sky. The stars shimmered brightly. He knew his constellations and found most of them. He thought he saw a shooting star. He couldn't be sure. His eyes might have been playing tricks on him. He was tired. A meteor, perhaps? Would a meteor count as lucky, too? Would God finally grant some luck, and maybe even guide them into that great city to end this horrible war? He didn't think so. All the luck seemed to have vanished after Gettysburg. Hudson looked at the city again through field glasses, but there really wasn't much to see. He wondered, though, if somewhere in that flickering glow Abraham Lincoln paced the White House, fretting over the threat Early's army posed.

Well, at least he had sort of seen Washington. He figured it was time to scoot back up the Potomac. He truly didn't believe Early was coming. No, it would soon be time to go back to Virginia, and the army would need to know what was going on along the Potomac above Washington. He could render that service. If the army was still in Maryland at all, that is. Hudson rode off into the night, back the way he'd come, feeling quite alone.

When he reached Great Falls he heard a horse whinny and he pulled up behind a tree. The Navy Colt was instantly in his hand. It was very dark and quiet. He could see the outline of the approaching horse. There had to be Federal patrols this close to the city, but this was s single horse, a single rider. Only one man. He cocked the pistol and aimed. Hudson's horse snorted, and then so did the approaching one. Hudson heard its hooves dig into the dirt. It was very close.

Then a soft voice: "Hudson? Is that you, lieutenant." Hudson didn't think a Federal patrol could know his name, but he kept the pistol pointed as the other horse drew close.

"Who are you?" Hudson said. He could now see the outline of the man.

"It *is* you," the man said. "I figured as much. It's Sergeant Willis, lieutenant. Can I come on in?"

"Slowly," Hudson said, still aiming the pistol.

The sergeant dismounted and led his horse to Hudson, who recognized him and lowered the pistol.

"How the hell did you find me?" Hudson said.

"Been asking myself that, too," Sgt. Willis said. "Dumb luck, I reckon. My horse knows yours. I come down the Monocacy, same as you."

Fool, Hudson thought, but he was happy to see the sergeant. "I might have been a yankee, sergeant. You should be more careful."

"The yanks have better things to do than gallop about in pitch dark."

"I hope you're right," Hudson said. "What news do you have? What's happening with the army? Where are they?"

"Well, sir, the by God army won't be far away come tomorrow."

"Really?" Hudson said. "I thought—"

"The yanks put up a real fight at the Monocacy, lieutenant. But John Gordon's boys whipped them anyway. They ran off toward Baltimore with their tails between their legs, and Old Jube plans to march down the pike tomorrow."

"Dear Jesus," Hudson said. "They're really coming?"

"They really are, lieutenant." He pointed behind him, into the darkness. "Hell, they ought to make Rockville tomorrow for sure."

Hudson dismounted and patted the head of his horse. The sergeant reached into his saddlebags.

"When did you eat last, lieutenant?"

Hudson had to think a moment. "This morning."

"Well, then this is your lucky day. I got ham, lieutenant. Real ham. Those boys back at the river gave it to me. Took it off a yankee wagon. Here, I wrapped some in paper for you."

Hudson took the ham and chewed happily. It had been a long day and he thought it the finest ham he'd ever eaten. The sergeant produced a brown bottle.

"They had whiskey on that wagon, too, lieutenant."

"Do you have any other surprises, Sgt. Willis?"

"Yeah, lieutenant. Our orders—straight from Gen. Early himself."

In his elation and hunger and fatigue, Hudson had forgotten to ask about orders. How Unprofessional, he thought, and he winced. He really was tired. Then suddenly he realized what the orders might be, and the enormity of it rolled over him like a wave.

"And what does the good general want us to do?"

"Find the way into Washington."

Early had granted his exhausted men four hours of sleep, and then he put them back on the march, as improbable as it seemed. When they had stopped he knew they absolutely must rest if they were to have a chance at all the next day. But time was running out. It was a gamble of supreme proportions. Were the men at their limit? Or did they have something left? The unrelenting heat had hit the troops hard. Many were in no real shape to fight. Would four hours bring them back from the walking dead? Yesterday's victory on the Monocacy—would it be enough spark to ignite the fire they needed to take Washington? Those questions kept Early from getting much sleep. He had prayed that his men slept every minute of their four hours.

There would be plenty of time for sleep in a yankee prison if the gambit failed, and there were plenty of officers who believed it would. Early knew what he faced: strong forts ringed the city, and word had come that the bulk of the federal VI Corps, sent by Grant, was being ferried up the Potomac. Early already had a taste of VI Corps back at the Monocacy. Its advance units under Wallace had fought very well indeed. Now it would be a horse race to Washington, and Early had less than 14,000 men, but there was an opportunity in this, and what he had might just be enough if he could get there first.

His troops seemed able to embrace the opportunity that morning. They woke up stiff, sweaty, and still tired, of course, and it was going to be another hot day; but a little sleep and some breakfast had restored them some. Many of them sensed that one more fight could decide the war. They were certainly ready for something to happen. What had begun as a nuisance raid had suddenly blossomed into a chance to end it all. When he crossed into Maryland Early had boasted that he would take Washington, but he hadn't truly believed it until he rode up and down ragged gray lines of infantry. With each rubbery step they made the city closer. If they could just keep forcing one foot in front of the other and beat VI Corps to the punch—yes, it was possible. He now believed. With God's blessing, of course. With God's help and a way to slip around those forts. He had a scout looking into that. Early prayed that God would guide that scout. Much depended on that man, a young and bright lieutenant. As Early rode among his men it occurred to him that he could not remember the scout's name. He hoped that was not a bad omen.

When the Army of the Valley reached the outskirts of Washington, Early learned that VI Corps was approaching the city docks. A decision had to be made. Having come this far, Early did not want to just give up and slink back into Virginia. His men were tired and hot, but they weren't beaten. There was a determination, a grittiness, that was strong in them. They knew the stakes and had seen victory snatched away too often. Some of them, a pitiful few, were Gettysburg veterans. That battle, too, was supposed to have been the last one.

The most exposed fort was Ft. Stevens, northeast of the city. Early surveyed the fort through field glasses and then looked grimly at his officers, who reminded him of lost sheep as they huddled together and waited for direction. He saw gray clumps of infantry all around, snatching a few more minutes of rest against trees and knapsacks. He studied them for signs of defeat. He didn't think he saw that, but there was no more time to juggle information. The decision begged to be made. Early wavered, felt himself weaken, loathed the feeling, but knew he was going to call it off when an officer rode up. It was the scout, the man he had sent off to find a way into Washington. The fate of the army—perhaps the Confederacy—now likely hinged on what he was told by a young lieutenant whose name escaped him.

The scout dismounted so swiftly that he nearly toppled onto the general, who returned the salute and said awkwardly, "Young man."

An aide whispered the scout's name into the general's ear.

"Hudson—yes. Lieutenant Hudson, of course." Early was relieved to finally know his name and seemed to prefer to prolong the exchange of pleasantries rather than face the harsh truth. "I sent a sergeant to find you. Is he well?"

"No, sir. He was killed by a patrol this morning. I barely escaped myself."

Early looked away, hands clasped behind his back. "I'm sorry about your man. I won't bore you with patriotic mumblings about sacrifice and duty. We both know the value of such things."

"Thank-you, sir," Hudson said. "I believe I have come to know the value of those things pretty well." He added "sir" after a long pause.

"I can imagine," Early said, and there was another pause. Ignoring the impertinence, he added, "What can you tell me, son? Did you find a way into the city? Is there a place where we might slip around those forts?"

"No, sir. There's no gap that I could see, and believe me, I got as close as sacrifice and duty would allow."

Early nearly smiled at the sharpness of the lieutenant's tongue, but instead he turned away again and prepared to send his army back into Virginia.

"But, sir," Hudson said, "you don't need a gap. Fort Stevens is defended only by an artillery battery."

Early whirled around. "You're sure of this?"

"Yes, sir. I saw it up close, and I spoke to civilians."

Early frowned. "Perhaps they lied to you. Yes, that's probably it. What else would they say to a Confederate officer?"

"General, I wore civilian clothes and told them I was a farmer looking for work. I hid my uniform in my saddlebags. Sir, right by God now that fort is held by one battery of artillery."

The general studied Hudson's face. He saw what he thought was earnestness ablaze in the young man's eyes.

A staff officer stepped forward. "Sir, we must be very careful here. This information is sketchy at best. We must not make a rash decision."

Early wiped his brow with his sleeve, then faced the officer. "Colonel, you heard the young man. Give the order. Move this army against Fort Stevens immediately."

On the words of a young lieutenant who no longer believed himself part of a righteous crusade, the Army of the Valley staggered forward with ebbing will and strength and overran Ft. Stevens. Now the horse race had truly begun. On the other side of the city VI Corps troopers were stepping off boats. Was Early too late? He looked around at his men. It was still a small army. A tired army. And he knew, awfully, that he could not long hold the city against VI Corps and whatever else Grant would send. He might only get a portion of the city. And Lee could not help him. Lee was far away, locked in his own misery against Grant. If Early was to succeed, he had to do it with what he had, and with whatever luck that came his way.

A column of captured Federals filed by, looks of surprise still on many of their faces. Early watched them a while, then it dawned on him, thunderously, and he immediately issued the order to stunned subordinates.

"Can we do this?" said a major.

"It's all that's left to us," Early said. "We must try."

A band of Confederate cavalry was brought up and they put on Federal uniforms taken from prisoners. Early spotted Hudson and waved him over.

"Lieutenant, have you been to Washington before?"

"No, sir. This is my first time."

"Well, don't worry—you'll be in good company. You ride with this cavalry. Find the White House. Can you do that, son?"

Hudson didn't know if he could, but heard himself say, "I can try, sir."

A cavalry officer spoke up: "But general, these ain't even cavalry uniforms."

"Then I suggest you don't tell anyone," Early said.

"General," Hudson said. "General, when we find the White House what do you want us to do?"

"Capture Abraham Lincoln."

As Hudson's horse clattered along Washington's streets, an officer riding alongside him said, "Do you think we'll be shot as spies if we're captured in these uniforms?"

"I've been wondering about that myself," Hudson said. "I reckon we better not get caught."

They rode their horses into a lather, stopping to ask questions of civilians who thought it odd for Yankee soldiers to need directions to the White House. One finely-dressed gentleman finally pointed his cane at them and said in a shrill voice, "The damn uniforms are all wrong. Why, that's an infantry blouse, and that's artillery."

"Yes, sir," Hudson said, tipping his hat. "Ours didn't come back from the laundry and those fellows were kind enough to loan us theirs."

"Well, you can't show up at the White House dressed like that," the man called after them as they galloped down the street.

The White House finally appeared. Hudson said they had but one chance in hell of success and so the motley gaggle of uniforms and lathered horses charged the White House grounds while Hudson yelled maniacally, "Let us pass, let us pass—we bear dispatches from the front."

The startled White House guards wondered why it took more than fifty men to deliver a message, but they were intimidated by Hudson's audacity and waved the band through. The Confederates overwhelmed the guards, who still weren't sure why men in blue uniforms were herding them away.

Hudson led his men from room to room, and in the end it was surprisingly low key: he opened a door, pistol drawn, more armed men crowding his shoulders, and came face to face with Abraham Lincoln.

"Dear Jesus," Hudson said as he stared up at Lincoln.

"I have been called far worse, young man. Would you care to sit down?"

Hudson and his men eased into the room. Several removed their hats self-consciously. All Hudson could think was how tall Lincoln was.

"Well, do you mind if *I* sit down?" Lincoln said, not waiting for a reply. "There, that's better. I needed to get off my feet a spell. Well, gentlemen, you got in. Now tell me—how do you plan to get out?"

It was a good question, and Hudson had thought of it, but his brain wasn't ready to ship an appropriate response down to his mouth.

"I'm a Confederate officer—sir!"

"Well, son, when I saw the drawn guns and mishmash of uniforms, I didn't think you had come to throw me a party."

Hudson left Lincoln under guard and went outside to check on the rest of his men. He noticed civilians who had witnessed the commotion and were now jockeying for a better look from across the street. None of them seemed to quite know what had happened. Several had started across the street toward Hudson. But they abruptly stopped and retreated. Hudson looked down the street and saw infantry approaching. He reached for his pistol, then realized they were gray infantry, not blue.

Confederate infantry swarmed like locusts over the White House grounds, but within minutes came under fire as VI Corps arrived and deployed. Word was sent to the Federals that Lincoln had been captured and was still in the White House. That stopped the firing. Early appeared and ordered Lincoln taken out of the city. Hudson went along as commander of the guard. Another message went to the Federals, exaggerating the size of Early's army and demanding that VI Corps either surrender or march itself back onto its boats and sail away because its back was to the Potomac and the Army of the Valley would burn Washington before it would surrender it.

A stalemate arose. As news of the capture of Lincoln and Washington spread, the already strong anti-war feelings in the war-weary North grew even more vocal. Gen. George McClellan attempted to take control of the Federal government but was stopped by forces loyal to Lincoln. Within weeks it was all over: the Federals agreed to an armistice with the Confederacy. Lincoln was released and established a temporary capital in Philadelphia. Less than a year later New York became the permanent capital. Washington became the Confederate capital, to the delight of Lee, who moved back to Arlington.

But Jefferson Davis, while visiting Washington just after the armistice, slipped and fell in front of Ford's Theatre, which featured a fine John Wilkes Booth performance that evening. Davis died in a house across the street. Lee reluctantly accepted the presidency. Littlefield Hudson went home to Virginia and became a teacher.

Confederate Nation was born.

Part I

Chapter 1

▼

Late Spring, 1999

It was sort of like driving into Canada. Or perhaps more like Franco's Spain. Smiling border guards, automatic weapons slung heavily over their shoulders, greeted tourists at the checkpoints, politely checked their U.S. passports, and cheerfully directed them to the nearest McDonald's, Taco Bell, or Jeff Davis Chicken Hut. It had been decades since the guards routinely confiscated anything mentioning Abraham Lincoln or Martin Luther King—or even New York Yankees bumper stickers. But however affable, these Confederate States of America border guards wore pearl gray uniforms and slouch hats remarkably suggestive of the ones worn by their infamous forefathers at Antietam, Chancellorsville, and Fredericksburg, and their sleeves proudly sported the Stars and Bars.

Canada with an attitude.

The last border incident was in 1975, when Ida Mae Simpson of Sharpsburg, Maryland, drove her sky blue Chevy Malibu over the Stonewall Jackson Bridge at Harper's Ferry and the accelerator stuck while she ordered a pizza on her cell phone. Mrs. Simpson crashed through the gates, clipped a guardhouse, and slid to a halt in a vacant lot next to a McDonald's on the Virginia side. One of the guards considered shooting out the Malibu's tires, but thought better of the idea, realizing Mrs. Simpson probably wasn't the spearhead of a Northern invasion. No one was hurt, and the guards served the rattled Mrs. Simpson coffee from Starbucks while she waited for a tow truck and her cousin Velma to come pick her up.

As Grail Hudson walked across the quad of the University of Illinois he remembered that he was just 16 and living with his mother in Kalamazoo, Michigan, at the time of Mrs. Simpson's accidental invasion of the C.S.A. Something in the very young faces that engulfed him and flooded the quad pathways transported him back to that time. Mrs. Simpson had only merited page four of the *Kalamazoo Gazette* because of coverage of the end of the Vietnam War. Just as in World War I, and World War II—Rommel had praised its tenacity—as well as Korea, a Confederate Legion had been raised to fight in Vietnam, although there were C.S.A. officials who grumbled that Vietnam, after all, was yet another conflict between a North and a South.

There was even a Robert E. Lee Brigade in Vietnam, a unit that dated back to the Normandy Invasion. When the Stars and Stripes were raised atop Mt. Suribachi on Iwo Jima, right next to them waved the Confederate battle flag. When Walter Cronkite reported from Vietnam that "C.S.A. troops today took a key hill from the Vietcong in the Ia Drang Valley," fluttering insolently behind Walter and the key hill were the Stars and Bars. Even though the C.S.A. and U.S.A. had long suffered different views on domestic policies, they were generally comfy cousins on foreign matters.

Mrs. Simpson's foray had ignited a passion inside Grail for all matters Confederate, tempered, of course, by his staunch devotion to the Union. But he was indeed a voyeur of that which made him uneasy, never a particularly effective barrier to choosing a career, and so at 17 he became a foreign exchange student for a semester at Jefferson Davis High School in Charleston, South Carolina. The school principal found Grail a bit peripatetic, but a talented writer of history. Unfortunately, Grail was a also a writer of graffiti, his talent in that area perhaps not so promising, because on a visit to Fort Sumter he spray-painted "Lee's a Queer!" and "The North Rules!" in bright orange on a wall of the fort and got punched by two loyal sons of the South, who also pitched into the bay the new loafers his Mom had sent him.

After that many a bright boy might have shifted his career focus to accounting, or maybe leisure studies, but Grail, oddly enough, figured he was on to something, his fat lip notwithstanding. He went back to Michigan, where his mother was an English teacher at his high school, and decided he would give college a try that fall. In his final summer of innocence he chased girls at the beaches in South Haven and cheered the Tigers in Detroit with his Uncle George, a pleasant alcoholic who had filled in as best he could for Grail's father, who had died while Grail was in his mother's womb.

Grail had become a professor of American and C.S.A history at Illinois, a decent school in a deliberately boring town surrounded by flatness, corn, and Republicanism. Some of his students—also deliberately dull—had never heard much about the Civil War. They were more concerned with cell phones and personal pagers, but Grail did have a student from Indiana who analyzed how the Dallas Cowboys became the first National Football League franchise in the C.S.A. It was far more interesting and complicated than even Grail had imagined because for the first time the NFL was dealing with a foreign country instead of the usual gang of greedy capitalists, and there had been strong sentiment among C.S.A. officials to see the team named the Dallas Rebels.

He paused before entering the History Building and surveyed the students, a happy sea of indifference, ignorant bliss, physical joy, and disaffection all blended together to create a patchwork of youth seething with hormones and the occasional analytical thoughts. Soon their fathers and mothers and little sisters and brothers would show up to help them move out of dormitories and apartments for the summer. It had been Grail's uncle, not his father, who had performed that ritualistic act of parental benevolence and authority when Grail was at the University of Michigan.

But he was a man now, he reassured himself, and men could go on, could march on and heal themselves of what was missing from the foggy past. Surely that was true. He always clung to that notion. After all, he had become somebody in the academic world. He had written a book, *Birth of a Rebel Nation*, that sold a lot of copies, that was hotly debated in *The New York Times* and *Washington Post*, and raised a few eyebrows, particularly in the C.S.A. At 40 he should have been content. He had a house with ivy snaking up its walls on a quiet and dignified street where ivy-covered walls were sort of social merit badges.

He reached his office, an old grand affair darkened by teak paneling, but illuminated nicely through French doors opening to a portico that no one used anymore, that was lately more splashed with pigeon droppings and shadows than the rich currents of conversation of the generations before the cell phone. Back when people actually spoke to each other face to face. Students didn't sit on porticos anymore, preferring the trees under the quad, where it was easier to smoke a joint and see the enemy approaching in plenty of time—warned, no doubt, by a scout armed with a cell phone from another part of the quad.

Grail gazed out the French doors, out past the granite portico and ashen shadows, out past the green quad dotted with students, past the stately buildings ringing it, his eyes reaching, perhaps, for miles across the soggy soybean fields and corn fields surrounding the town, silent, wavy reminders that this was still a tight-assed, conservative, agricultural burg that merely tolerated the extravagances of the mind the university propagated, and he saw fog, though there was none in any sense of reality because it was a sunny day. But he saw fog because his far-reaching gaze had finally converged with his thoughts and he was seeing his father, what could be seen, that is, of a man who never really existed, a man he never knew and could not really know. He simply had no clue about the man. No pictures of him survived a fire, a very odd thing at that, and Grail's mother claimed none were taken of them during the short time they were married. Even odder.

She never said much about the man, her silence speaking volumes instead, and Grail sensed a pain in her emanating somehow from his father, and that complicated Grail's need to know the man. Grail could only be sure that Lewis Hudson had been six feet tall, possessed piercing blue eyes, and light brown hair. He had worked in a Detroit machine shop and was just twenty-one when he drowned in Lake Erie south of Detroit while boating with friends. He left behind no image or memory upon which Grail could dream and wonder.

Chapter 2

▼

When Grail did dream, his father was a whiff of smoke. No human form, just undulating, foggy vapor. It was Robert E. Lee that came to him in the flesh. And way too much flesh at that: lately the old general was showing up in a g-string. Studded with rhinestones. Despite an alabaster "body" devoid of any discernible muscle, Lee looked vaguely like a member of The Village People. After a few dreams Lee appeared one night in a red silk kimono emblazoned with dragons spewing flames.

"A nice Japanese fellow loaned it to me," Lee said. "I thought you might be more comfortable seeing me in this."

"The g-string was quite a fashion statement," Grail said.

"Of course it wasn't real," said Lee, who was sitting, but to Grail it appeared that the old general was sitting on air.

"The g-string?" Grail said.

"Yes," Lee said. "How I appear is up to you. It's your dream, after all."

Grail was uneasy about that. At his office on campus he occasionally found himself analyzing it. During student conferences his mind would drift as he pondered it. Why did he see Lee in a g-string? He was glad for the kimono, and some nights the general wore different colored kimonos. Grail's favorite was the blue one with snakes descending from the shoulders. It made the general look younger. Grail concluded that the g-string's demise was a good thing, maybe even resolution of some subconscious conflict. He just wished he knew what it was that he'd figured out. But he was especially relieved that he never saw the smoke that was his father in a g-string.

In one dream Lee hinted about the nature of the hereafter.

"Are you in heaven?" Grail asked. "You were always considered a demi-God, after all."

"The adulation was embarrassing. And it wouldn't go away. I didn't want it."

"So, are you in heaven?"

"Well, it's not a bad place, I can tell you that. A lot of interesting people."

"What about dreams?" Grail said. "What's the deal on dreams?"

"Perplexing, aren't they?" Lee said. "I always thought so. Of course, I never put anyone in a g-string I might tell you."

"Sorry about that," Grail said.

"It's OK," Lee said. "Times change."

"So, give me a hint about dreams. Do we leave our bodies?"

"Sort of. Your essence, who you really are, gets closer to what we call up here the ultimate level of existence. Is that vague enough?"

"Absolutely. So, how's General Grant doing?"

"Dressing better than when I saw him at Appomattox."

"You see him often?"

"We play checkers every Thursday night."

"You still use days of the week up there?"

"Gives the place some structure."

"I see. How's Grant's drinking?"

"He says that was overblown. There's no whiskey here."

"How does he cope?"

"He plays a lot of checkers."

If he seemed to be in a good mood Lee would entertain a few questions about Gettysburg, but if Grail pressed the issue too much—especially if he brought up Longstreet's pleas for a flanking attack around the Union right—he became defensive. He said he ran into Longstreet occasionally, and though they both tried hard to be friendly there was an awkwardness to their encounters. Longstreet insisted always on wearing the uniform of a Confederate lieutenant general, while Lee had long since abandoned the gray uniform for kimonos.

Sometimes Lee got up abruptly from his seat on air, resolutely tightened the sash of his kimono, and faded into fog. At least that's what Grail thought it was. Heaven seemed pretty foggy. And at the end of every dream, as Grail began to wake up, reality slinking slowly back into his brain, the last image was always the smoke that was his father.

Chapter 3

▼

A week into the dreams Grail visited a psychology professor he'd met at a faculty reception. The man was drumming up votes for some boring faculty senate resolution that Grail couldn't recall, but he figured his vote was enough leverage to get some free couch time. Grail didn't want to actually go to a shrink if he could avoid it, and to his relief Dr. Richard Ewell believed that the dreams, however exotic, were probably healthy. The g-string, Ewell conceded, was a bit dramatic; but he felt the silk kimonos indicated Grail's growing acceptance of Lee after first stripping him of dignity by putting him in the skimpy g-string.

"And you say it was studded with rhinestones, too?"

"Big red and green ones," Grail said. "Rubies and emeralds, I suppose. It was quite a beauty. As g-string go, that is."

"Well, I can't imagine it flattered the man much, from what I remember of Lee in history books," Dr. Ewell said. He pulled a pipe from his desk's center drawer, filled it, and fired it up, puffing deeply to get it going. The gray smoke curled toward the ceiling of his office and partly hid his white-bearded face from Grail. The smoke made him think of his father again, but he let the thought pass.

"Dr. Ewell—"

"Please, call me Richard. We're colleagues. Just different departments."

"Right. Of course. Did you know, Richard—and I just realized this myself—your name is the same as one of Lee's corps commanders at Gettysburg?"

"Really?" Ewell said, puffing away at the pipe. "Hmmm."

It was a professional "hmmm," not a social "hmmm," and Grail detected the difference.

"Was the man competent?" Ewell said, feverishly puffing at the pipe. The smoke looked like a tiny tornado funnel spinning a huge plume up along the cracked ceiling.

"I'm afraid he was disappointing at Gettysburg. He failed to take a key hill."

Ewell uttered another hmmm. "A bad day, perhaps?"

"Perhaps," Grail said. "Gettysburg was a bad day all round for Confederate generals."

And then Grail explained about the smoke that was his father. It was in all his dreams. Sometimes the smoke was pure white, other times it was green, red, purple, yellow; and even sometimes it was a collage of many colors that glowed like a Christmas tree. The form never varied. It always appeared as a sort of dancing, six-foot letter t. Although sometimes it seemed to ooze more than dance. Sometimes it just shuffled. Sometimes it appeared to wave to him. Always it was there just after Lee faded into nothing and Grail woke up.

"And you've never even seen a photograph of your father? That's peculiar." Ewell puffed furiously at the pipe. Grail looked up at the ceiling, which was barely visible through the haze. He wondered if Ewell might puff himself into an explosion, the force of the blast propelling him through the ceiling and out of sight into the heavens.

"And you see this smoke in every dream about Lee?"

"At the end, after Lee has gone and I'm about to wake up," Grail said. "What do you suppose it means?"

"It can mean many things." His pipe had gone out and he labored to light it again. He got it going and more smoke curled toward the ceiling. Grail checked to see if it resembled a six-foot letter t, but it was just regular smoke.

"For example?" Grail said.

"Well, it seems you have two fathers, essentially."

"Two?"

"Exactly. Lee is your dream father, which is appropriate enough because you never knew him. And yet you do because he is a prominent figure in your field. Your real father appears at the end of your dreams when you are coming back to reality because even though you didn't know him, either, he's the real deal, so to speak."

"I suppose you're right," Grail said, not convinced. "Why do you think I had to strip Lee of dignity?"

"You tell me," Ewell said, puffing away at the pipe. "Do you dislike the man? I don't know all that much about Robert E. Lee, but you're the expert. What was he really like?"

Grail pondered that a moment. Ewell's gaze was penetrating, the pipe jammed into his mouth making him appear more determined. He was Sherlock Holmes hard on the heels of Grail's ghosts. But he was generating an awful lot of smoke. It filled Grail's nostrils. He wasn't a smoker.

"Lee was an elitist," Grail finally said, trying not to cough. "And he once wrote that things tended to fall apart wherever there were black people. Words to that effect. He was a racist, too, although a subtle enough racist."

"Which is most problematic to you, elitism or racism?" Ewell said.

That was a good question, Grail admitted to himself. Elitism, it would seem, should naturally create racism. Could that be absolutely so? Could someone be an elitist but not a racist? Perhaps so. Theoretically, an elite socioeconomic group could be multi-racial and therefore race would be irrelevant to becoming elite. Maybe not. Republicans consider themselves the rightful elite of the U.S., but they're hardly a diverse, accommodating bunch. Yes, the question was a good one, but Grail didn't want to pursue it. The setting was wrong, the atmosphere just not right. A clinical examination wasn't what he wanted after all.

"So, Richard, how about a beer? Let's go have a drink."

"A beer?" Ewell said, frowning as though Grail had suggested a frontal lobotomy.

"Yes, Dick. A beer. More specifically a Sierra Nevada. Or a Bell's Amber Ale."

"I really prefer Richard, if you don't mind."

"I don't mind at all. What I sort of mind, but no offense intended, Richard, is sitting in this office and watching it fill up with smoke and perhaps the fire department showing up with huge hoses. And since I imposed by dropping in, and now I want to change the venue, I think I should at least buy. So, a beer?"

"Well, I—"

"C'mon, Richard. You're probably done for the day, right? Let's have a laugh. We can talk about elitism over a brewski. And you're faculty resolution."

Ewell's face brightened. He put the pipe in an ashtray. "Smoking often helps me concentrate. Sorry if it was too much."

"It's really ok," Grail said.

Ewell stood up. "Where do you suggest?"

"Murphy's Pub? It's close."

As they left Grail stole a glance over his shoulder at the buildup of smoke along the ceiling. He checked for signs of a six-foot letter t, but it was just regular smoke and did not wave to him.

The ceiling of Murphy's Pub was alive with whirling fans. So many that Grail thought the roof should just peel back so the bar could lift off into the stratosphere. There was a good amount of breeze and that made it impossible for smoke to collect, which made Grail feel better. They sat at the bar, a narrow sea of initials carved into the wood surface, and Ewell, who clearly did not spend much time in bars, had the nearly giddy look of a man suddenly thrust into the jaws of adventure and discovering he enjoyed it.

"It's been ages since I've done this," Ewell said, tipping his pint of Guinness toward Grail in salute.

"To reviving old vices," Grail said, taking a sip of Bell's. His beer was very cold and spicy.

The bartender, a pretty young student with a ring in her nose and blond hair piled atop her head, put coasters under their beers. Ewell attempted a conversation with her, revealing that he didn't really know how to talk to students outside a classroom. She wore a top that exposed her midriff, and he seemed transfixed by the circle tattooed around her bellybutton.

"I'm not sure I'll ever understand this obsession with tattoos," Ewell said after she had gone to the other end of the bar.

"It's their thing, I guess," Grail said. "That and piercings. It defines them, but I'm not sure that's a good thing. It seems insubstantial. Style over substance. How do you like her nose ring?"

Ewell tried to suppress a smile. "There's something sensual about that."

"I know, and that's just a nose ring. God knows where else she's got one."

Ewell gazed down the long bar and studied the girl. Her jeans were very tight. "Do you think so?"

"Wouldn't surprise me at all," Grail said.

"Have you seen one?" Ewell said, checking to see where the bartender was. "Up close, I mean." His voice had dropped to a whisper.

Grail hesitated, drank a gulp of the cold Bell's. It was so cold it hurt his head for a moment. "Yes. Yes, I have."

Ewell grinned and raised his beer. "Here's to unexpected objects in anatomy class."

Laughing, Grail clinked his glass against Ewell's, and chugged the rest of his beer.

They were feeling the beer. The bartender came back and asked if they needed anything. They smirked, looked awkwardly at each other and the girl before ordering more beer. Her expression never changed. Grail thought she looked bored. Maybe she was just tired of men mentally undressing her. Or immune to it from experience. She brought them two more pints but was smiling now and said "enjoy." You never knew about women, Grail thought. But then, they must think the same about us. It's a mystery that we come together for anything substantial, but we do sometimes, with a little luck and a lot of patience. But it's so tough, and often as not nothing comes of it at all.

"Richard," he said. "Richard, let me ask you something." He sipped his beer. "I want to ask your opinion on something."

"Fire away."

"Do you believe in reincarnation?"

"I believe in Guinness beer," Ewell said and downed another gulp.

"I'm serious," Grail said. "Do you believe in it?"

"Where's this coming from, Grail? By the way, I have meant to comment on your name. Most unusual. I've never met a Grail before. Here's to the Grails of the world, holy or not." He chugged some more Guinness, his face wet with foam.

"Seriously, Richard—and my vote for your resolution may hang in the balance—do you believe in reincarnation?"

"No. No, I really don't."

"What do you believe?"

"I was born and raised a Catholic, Grail. To make my family happy, and now my wife, I go to church and go through the motions. But if you want to know what I believe, it's pretty simple. I think at some point in every life the lights begin to dim and then one day they shut off altogether and that's that. I wish I could be more reassuring."

Grail frowned, looked away and then back at Ewell. "Nothingness, then—fade to black."

"Essentially," Ewell said. "No pearly gates, no edenic paradise."

"Do you ever hope you're wrong?"

"Sure. All the damn time. It's just that I never really see any hard evidence to change my mind. Do you believe in it—reincarnation?"

Grail thought hard, drummed his fingers on the bar, felt Ewell's penetrating gaze, an infinite sea of patience damned up behind it, and ordered another round. "Yeah. Yes. I do. Don't ask me how or why. I just do. A gut feeling. Or if not reincarnation, then something. Something else to go to. The human spirit, I mean. It has another existence. I just feel it. What it is, though, I don't know."

"Here's to Grail Hudson's theory of the human spirit," Ewell said after the beers had arrived. He held his mug high and winked at Grail. "Say, I've meant to ask you about all this talk I hear in the papers about reunification. You're the

C.S.A. expert. Will we reunite with out southern cousins? The *New York Times* barely misses a day without some opinion piece predicting the day is almost here."

"You believe it?" Grail said.

"I don't know. But then I never thought the Berlin Wall would come down, so you just never know anymore. But *you* must be watching it pretty closely."

"Of course," Grail lied. But the truth was otherwise. Between the dreams of Robert E. Lee, his anxieties over his father, the classes he taught, and his romance with a graduate student named Darla Pinsky from Mt. Pleasant, Michigan, Grail was out of touch.

"As they say, Rome didn't fall in a day," Grail said. "No, I think it's safe to say these things build for a long time, like the pressure that makes a diamond. It takes an eternity sometimes."

"Yeah," Ewell said, "but it's already been 135 years. Hasn't there been reunification talk almost from the day the war ended back in 1864?"

Grail nodded, but admitted to himself he should have paid more attention the past year. Could he be wrong? Maybe—no, he was a scholar, preeminent in his field. He probably was not wrong. Probably not. Likely there was time for him to get back to the reunification watch, to be ready to interpret it whenever, if ever, it finally came to pass.

"I think it's safe to say that the New York Times is guilty of a little wishful thinking," Grail said, reaching for his mug. He took a big gulp and swiveled on his stool to face Ewell. "No reunification. Not this year, anyway."

Chapter 4

▼

When Grail was nine he watched a schooner sink off South Haven, Michigan. It sank slowly and sadly, as though reluctant to end so fine a life of effortless leaps and dashes across deep blue water. The schooner was out of Petoskey, rich incompetents at the helm, and bound for Chicago before a squall and too many vodka gimlets panicked the crew into a mistake. The furled sails were white and one of the heavy masts snapped as the schooner slipped awkwardly beneath the waves. Grail walked out the long concrete pier toward the lighthouse for a better view. He had just arrived from Kalamazoo to swim at the beach, but now he was afraid to go into the water. He could see people from the schooner frantically thrashing in orange life jackets as white caps crashed over them. They waved their arms and Grail knew they must be yelling, must be screaming, but a wind had come up and they were too far away to be heard.

The Coast Guard fished out the survivors and Grail watched as they shivered and huddled under blankets on the pier. The water was cold, even in summer, and the survivors were wild-eyed, their hair matted. A fat man wearing only Bermuda shorts under his blanket tried to walk but his legs were wobbly and Grail thought the cold must have frozen his legs a little. Later he heard the man had been drunk and his wife had a broken arm from when he pushed her aside to jump out of the schooner. A Coast Guard officer in a brilliant white uniform told them all how close they had come to becoming drowned souls. The fat man sat down hard on the pier and vomited. His wife turned away and cradled her arm. She glanced once at Grail and then nervously at her broken arm. He had never seen anyone look so scared.

Grail tried to imagine the schooner on the bottom of the lake. Had it landed upright or turned over? He had just read in school that the Titanic landed upright, as though it were just sailing along the bottom of the bitter cold North Atlantic. He pictured that for a while and then tried to imagine the drowned people from the Titanic. Did they still inhabit the decks as ghosts while the ship rode the ocean floor? Where do drowned bodies go? What happens to them? Do fish eat them? He tried to imagine Lewis Hudson, his father, drowned at the bottom of Lake Erie. He had not been on a ship or even a schooner, just a small motorboat. Where did his body go? Where did they all go, the drowned souls? Did the people from the Titanic get sucked into the Gulfstream and wind up in Cuba? He wasn't sure where the Gulfstream was, but thought vaguely it might have something to do with the Titanic.

"You shouldn't worry about things like that," his mother said in the car on the way back to Kalamazoo. "It's not important where the body goes. Once someone is dead the body doesn't mean anything. The soul leaves the body when someone dies."

After a while Grail said, "When?"

His mother gave him a puzzled look. "When? What do you mean?"

"When does the soul leave the body? How does it know when to leave?"

Grail saw his mother chew her lip and wipe strands of brunette hair from her face. She looked back at him several times, but neither one said anything until they stopped at a gas station at Bangor and she bought Grail a Grape Nehi. They sat on a bench outside the station and watched the traffic to Kalamazoo zip by. She drank a Seven-Up and then hugged Grail.

"God tells the soul when it's time to go. Do you remember Reverend Thomas talking about the soul at church last week?"

"Yes."

"Well, when it's time, God guides the soul to the hereafter."

"Even if the body is under water?"

"No matter where the body is, God guides the soul."

"All those people on the Titanic?"

"Yes, all those poor people."

"God was busy that day, huh, Mom?"

"Yes. Yes, he was."

Grail felt a little better after their talk, but a few miles down the road when they crossed the Paw Paw River the green flash of water through the guardrails made him think about drowned souls again and he tried very hard to imagine how God did it. He pictured God guiding his father's soul out of Lake Erie into the air and over Detroit's skyscrapers, and then guiding it somewhere north because that's where he figured the hereafter was—some place very north. But he couldn't picture a soul exactly. It always came out like a ghost from a scary movie on television. He had never seen his father or seen a picture of him because there weren't any, and that made it even harder. He didn't know if the soul resembled the body, which certainly wasn't much help because he had no image of the man in his head.

The drive home was warm and halfway he fell asleep leaning against his mother. He dreamed about hundreds of drowned souls flying north from where the Titanic sank. Great flocks of them. They looked like birds with people faces and flew very well, even though they had no wings and didn't even flap their arms. How did they do it? Where was God in all this? Grail supposed they would wait for his father when he arrived all those years later, but when he awoke he wasn't sure at all.

Chapter 5

▼

It was early morning, the radio turned down low, and so the news didn't sink in right away as Grail watched his hand trace the soft curves of Darla Pinsky's naked butt.

"OK, so you saw a ship sink when you were nine," she said lazily. "What does that—"

"Good Christ," Grail said. "Did I hear that right? Reach over and turn up the radio."

"Forget the radio," she said. "Put your hand back between my cheeks and I'll do anything you want."

He slid across her to the nightstand and turned up the radio. He had heard it right.

"Christ, Hudson—reunification," she said as she fumbled in her purse for a cigarette. She always called him Hudson.

Grail went over to the window and looked out at the red morning sky. Blood red. Red sky in morning, sailor take warning. He remembered that saying from childhood. Down on the corner people were waiting reasonably for a bus. Across the street Tom Fletcher in a paisley robe retrieved the *Champaign Courier* from his porch. Despite the news, the world apparently wasn't spinning off its axis. Just two weeks earlier he had told Richard Ewell reunification would not happen. Grail turned back to Darla. She had slipped out of her t-shirt.

"It's these or reunification," she said, lightly pinching her nipples. "Which one do you want to obsess about?"

"No contest," he said. He jumped back into bed and Darla slid on top of him. She filled his face with flesh and nipples, but soon he had to admit he was wrong.

The Union apparently was to be restored and that was bigger than breasts, bigger than sex—bigger even than Elvis Presley. He mumbled about it through her breasts and she slid off.

"Ok, I know they can't compete with history," she said, returning to her cigarette. The nipples were still very erect.

"It's reunification, Darla. After 135 years. This changes everything."

"I know." She blew rings of smoke at him. "I know that I'll probably have to change my thesis."

"It *has* to be your thesis."

"Yeah—mine and everybody else's. But the real question, Mr. Confederacy expert, is what are *you* going to do? You'll probably have to develop a new undergraduate course, right? Maybe a graduate seminar. Of course, that's after you go south. That's what you should do, Hudson—go down there and watch the paint dry."

"Do you think so?" He was still stunned by the news. "I don't know. Negotiations could take months. Maybe longer." He slid off the bed and went to brush his teeth. "You know," he called from the bathroom, "historians seem better suited to sifting through the cold remains instead of watching a thing crumble."

"Don't be lame, Hudson. Where's your motivation? What about Washington? Will it be the capital again?"

He stuck his head out of the bathroom door. "Could be. That way the Confederacy could sort of make amends for its capture. I don't know. It's complicated. There could be something that prevents that. Something political we don't know yet."

"See, Hudson? Now you're back to thinking like a historian."

In the shower Grail wondered why he had been reluctant when Darla suggested he witness reunification. Fear, he supposed. Fear that he had gotten stale, that he was better suited to drilling history into thick undergraduate skulls and a handful of idealistic graduate ones than to leap into history being manufactured, and to define it and predict its consequences without dusty books to provide a clue. After all, the future is just history that hasn't been written down yet.

He slipped on Levi's and a Michigan football sweatshirt—Grail enjoyed pissing off the locals—and went downstairs, but Darla had left for morning classes. He could still smell her in the house as he made coffee. He pulled an atlas from a drawer and spread it on the kitchen table. The borders of the C. S. A. were highlighted in black magic marker. Grail traced his finger along the border, spoke the names of the border states softly to himself. It didn't seem real yet that this foreign country, part of the union so long ago, was coming back into the fold. What was the price? Grail knew there was always a price in these things. What does the C.S.A. want? What does the U.S.A. want? Where's the payoff for both nations?

Maybe it will be an easy reunion, he thought as he sipped the coffee. Maybe not. But the C.S.A. had reformed a great deal over the years. Slavery, to the surprise of many, ended not long after the end of the Civil War, what C.S.A. history books refer to as The Great Patriotic War. Militant southerners reluctantly came to their senses and realized there could be no meaningful trade and relations with Europe as long as slavery existed. Longstreet and Lee knew as much even as they fought to establish the country. African-Americans were finally allowed to resettle into the C.S.A. in the early 1950s, though not without the inevitable conflicts, some violent, but the C.S.A. government resolved to reform itself and African-American senators and representatives appeared in its Congress by the late 1960s. The two countries have co-existed peacefully, cooperated in trade, and the current C.S.A. president, an aging but still vital Jimmy Carter is widely hailed as a fair man.

Grail took his coffee out to the deck behind the house, to the little garden of mostly flowers, a patch of tomato plants and even a few scraggly stalks of corn. The garden is where Grail went for privacy, to think. Now was his favorite time in the garden, spring, the air crisp and the sun playfully warm. In the garden Grail has learned the difference between the calls of bluejays and doves, and at dusk bats bank and swoop against the darkening sky. There is very little of modern life and its contraptions and annoyances to distract him, and in this solitude Grail tried to fathom the unfathomable: life, death, and the bittersweet mystery connecting them.

But it was not tragic in the garden. Grail always felt there was as much hope there as anything else. On his first date with Darla he had taken her there, to share his most sacred privacy, he supposed. That afternoon he had gone to Jupiter's, a downtown bar, to eat lunch and read the newspaper. Darla came in with some other graduate students, noticed him at the bar, and kept looking his way. The two of them had been running into each other for weeks, finally talked, and discovered they were both from Michigan.

At first Grail thought it was no more than just the standard infatuation with a professor he had endured from other graduate students. Some had romance on their minds, but many of them were merely looking for a father figure or an inside track to better grades. It finally occurred to him, though, that he and Darla were trading glances and smiles. There was chemistry between them. She was past 30, he knew, or rather, had made the effort to find out, and he was 40, an age difference he found desirable, so he sent a round of drinks over to her table as camouflage for cutting her out of the herd. He figured she would be the one to make the next move, would feel obligated to come over and thank him. She made him wait a few minutes—a little longer than he was comfortable with—to test his confidence, and then she strolled over slowly, with a wicked smile on her face.

"Don't mention it," Grail said. "It's the least I can do for a bunch of overworked graduate students."

"Don't forget underpaid and underappreciated," she said. "Is this your hangout."

"Only grad students have hangouts."

"What do professors have?"

"Tenure."

"Of course," she said, laughing softly. "Very clever. Tenure is Latin for godlike, isn't it?" Her smile lit up her face and for the first time Grail noticed how lovely the smile made her face become. Her eyes were green, also a new discovery for him, and her auburn hair fell on her shoulders with a hint of curl. There was a challenge in this. She was pushing ever so carefully but firmly.

"Will they miss you?" Grail said. He gestured over at her table, where the others were checking them out. "Can you stay a while?"

"Do you want me to stay?" Her voice was lower. Grail liked the touch of huskiness. She sounded a little like Lauren Bacall. "Yes. Yes, I want you to stay."

"Then go over and get my drink, will you?"

"Really?" he said.

"The humility will do you good." She had inched closer to him. Her eyes had an altogether new look—the pupils appeared somehow brighter, larger. And it excited Grail very much.

"You think I won't go over there?"

"I think they're already talking about us, so why not?"

"Good point." He went over and made small talk for a minute and came back with her drink.

"Thanks," she said, and for a moment she couldn't look at him, then she recovered.

"What do I call you?" she said.

"Waiter?"

"Funny," she said, but she clearly enjoyed the banter." I mean, I can't call you professor now that you're fetching my fricking drinks."

"Another graduate student dilemma," he said.

"Yes it is." She hesitated, looked away once, and took a sip from her drink. "I guess I call you Grail, don't I. It's an unusual name"

"You don't like it?" he said.

"I do like it. But it's unusual. How did you get it?"

"My Mom's a teacher. She studied the crusades and out of that somehow I became Grail."

"It suits you. There's a touch of the crusades about you."

"Oh, really?" he said. "Now I wonder what that might mean."

"Relax, big boy—I'm just jerking your chain a little."

"I noticed."

"Oh, are you touchy? I better find out these things before I get in too deep."

"How deep were you planning on?"

"Buy me another drink and I might tell you."

The bartender brought her a vodka gimlet. "Here's to the crusades," she said, clinking her glass against his. "What I meant a minute ago is that you are dramatic sometimes. That comes out in your classes, you know."

Grail sipped some of his beer and thought about it. "I didn't know. How do you mean?"

"You're passionate when you speak—demonstrative."

"Demonstrative?"

"You wave your arms a lot."

"I wave my arms? What am I, a bird?"

"Don't worry—it's endearing."

Darla slipped away to the ladies room. The other students came over to the bar to thank Grail again for the drinks, but mostly they wanted to smirk and make him feel uncomfortable about Darla. Grail knew it would get around soon enough, but he didn't care. Instead, he tried to picture himself waving his arms in class. Did he look like a bird that couldn't get off the ground? A dodo, maybe. Or maybe the arm waving was s some sort of sign of rebellion. He vaguely hoped so and tried to imagine what people might say: "Dr. Hudson's a rebel. He waves his arms in class and sleeps with graduate students." He was a little surprised to realize he enjoyed the image.

Darla came back and glanced over at the empty table where her friends had been.

"They said they were headed to The Esquire," Grail said. "They said to tell you good luck. Will you need it?"

"I just might," she said. "Was it traumatic when they came over?"

"Not at all. They invited us along, but I just told them we were going home to my place."

She blinked. "You didn't."

Grail paused, enjoyed the drama. "No, of course not. But it's a good idea. Let's go sit out on my deck and have another drink. I'll show off my little garden and you'll be impressed with how earthy I am."

"Will I pluck an apple for you to nibble on?"

"I don't have an apple tree. How about an ear of corn?"

"Screws up the symbolism," she said. "Has to be an apple."

"No problem. We'll go by the store and get apples and a bottle of something red or white, or both."

Darla smiled, mulled it over. For a long moment they were just two faces side by side in the mirror behind the bar.

"Well, Hudson, can I trust you?"

Now it was his turn to mull it over. "Sure," he said to her face in the glass. "After all, I'm named after the Holy Grail."

Chapter 6

▼

Restoring the Union had become the daily topic for real people as well as Oprah, Regis, Maury, Montell, and all the other self-appointed television gods practicing psychiatry without a license. Leno and Letterman skewered it nightly. The talking heads on TV analyzed it daily. Madonna wrote a song about it. The North-South football game was renamed the Reunification Bowl.

Grail witnessed in disbelief as reunification unfolded on the TV in his office. He watched as presidents Carter and Clinton jogged together between press conferences. Foreign dignitaries shuttled between New York and Washington to give their blessings and curry favor. Fidel Castro sent the two presidents cigars. Even Moamar Ghadaffi sent a basket of fruit, which was thoroughly searched and tested. Saddam Hussein said reunification, of course, was a Zionist plot, but most of the rest of the world applauded the impending reunion of the two Americas.

The actual ceremony to make reunification official, a state dinner and dance hosted by Carter in Washington, was just weeks away. The process had been consummated as swift as a forest fire, with few disagreements between the U.S.A. and C.S.A. to iron out. The two presidents played golf and smoothed out the problems between holes. The two countries were clearly eager to be one again after so many years as cozy cousins. Even 64-year-old Elvis Presley agreed to come out of semi-retirement to sing at the reunification ball.

It was all enough to make Grail dizzy. He gazed numbly at the TV and shook his head at how badly he had underestimated the road to Union. He would not make the mistake again of being so consumed with teaching and his own problems that he would miss something so important to his field. But he had to admit to himself that he wasn't sure what he should do to inject himself back onto the national stage as a CSA expert. Darla had said go down there and watch the paint dry. Sure. But he was rusty and needed motivation, a spark—something dramatic to help him see what he should do.

Grail was so transfixed by the events on TV he didn't immediately notice a smiling Kendra Remington, head of his department, leaning against his door, arms crossed, watching him in his stupor.

"What are you going to do about it?" she said.

He looked up and stared a moment, could not immediately make words form in his mouth. "About reunification?"

"No, Britney Spears' belly button. Yes—reunification." Grail shrugged, got up to stretch. "Even Geraldo Rivera knew it before me. Pretty sad."

"By the way," she said, "how is that graduate student you go out with—what's her name? Britney Lipinsky, something like that?"

"Darla Pinsky. So, you know about that." He felt faintly scolded and sat down.

"Everybody knows about that, Grail."

"Really?" He hadn't thought his life was so public. "Well, you know, she's not in any of my classes, and she's not one of the little 21-year-olds, so—" Kendra put up her hand. "Take it easy, Grail. Nobody cares whether you go out with Britney Spears."

"Darla Pinsky. What does everybody care about?"

"Forget what other people think," she said, leaning closer to his desk. "I got a call yesterday from Paul Klaussen. We were at Northwestern together. Now he's at Virginia. Have you heard of him?"

"No, I can't say I know him."

"He read your book on the C.S.A., and that recent New Yorker piece."

"It's nice to have fans. What's his specialty?"

"Same as yours, except he's a southern boy, of course."

"Why did he call—to nitpick something, to defend the honor of Robert E. Lee?"

"Not at all. He said he loved the book and article."

"So?"

"So, he called with some rather interesting news. It seems Virginia is all agog over the recent discovery of a Confederate officer's long lost diary."

"Really?" Grail said. "Robert E. Lee's secret kinky diary, I hope. Nights of bondage with Jeff Davis and James Longstreet."

"Nothing so exotic, I'm afraid. But you might be interested in the officer's name—Littlefield Hudson."

Grail leaned back in his chair a bit and studied Kendra's face. No doubt she expected some reaction from him. "I know about him. He captured Lincoln. A historical footnote."

"Did you know he wrote a diary?"

"No. Evidently he kept it secret. He became a teacher after the war and worked hard to disassociate himself from the Confederacy. The diary would be interesting to see, of course. Especially if he wrote down his thoughts on capturing Lincoln."

"Klaussen said he did. Excited?"

"Intrigued," Grail said. "I'll get excited if it opens some new doors."

"That may be the case."

"How so?"

"Klaussen poked around the Hudson family tree in Virginia and it seems that one of Littlefield's sons moved to Detroit around 1890. Paul knew from your book that you're from Michigan, so he called me."

"I see," Grail said, expelling a long sigh. "He hopes we're related."

"Of course he does," she said. "It's natural enough, don't you think?"

"Yeah, I suppose. Sure. But we're not related."

"You're so sure?"

"There are plenty of Hudsons walking around Detroit. It's coincidental. Besides, I was born in Monroe, south of Detroit."

Kendra smiled and shook her head. "You're touchy about this, and I know why. You're afraid of how it would look—you, a staunch Northerner and critic of the C.S.A. suddenly revealed to be related to the man who captured Lincoln."

It was true enough, Grail admitted to himself, if he was related, but he knew of no evidence linking him to Littlefield Hudson. Certainly it had never been suggested by his family.

"I'm not touchy, Kendra. Klaussen is barking up the wrong family tree."

"Ok," she said. "But you'll call him, right? The diary may be of some value to your research."

"I will call Mr. Klaussen."

"And be civil. He's an old friend."

"I'll call this afternoon and be charming."

She got up to leave, but stopped in the doorway. "You know, it wouldn't be so bad, would it? To be related to Littlefield Hudson? You said he abandoned Confederate principles. That's a good thing."

"I suppose so," Grail said, just hoping she would drop the subject and leave, but he realized he wasn't quite done, either. "It's good that Littlefield Hudson wised up on slavery and secession. Very admirable. But he did wear the uniform to the bitter end. You might even say he was the architect of the last 135 years. Is that a good thing? Or was he sort of like the Nazis, who said they were merely following orders?"

She nodded. "Sounds like a new book."

"I'll get right on that," he said as she disappeared out his door.

But instead Grail put his feet up on his desk, his hands behind his head, and watched TV, still a little flummoxed about reunification. After a while his thoughts drifted and soon he wondered about Littlefield Hudson's son, the one that migrated to Detroit. Did he have children of his own? Did their descendants still live in Detroit? Should he go there and find them? Ask how they feel about reunification? Maybe that was his angle in all this. That might be the way to jumpstart a new book, to begin at the beginning—Littlefield was the beginning, and his descendants the logical place to start. If there were any descendants. But surely there were. He would try and find them, see what their story was.

He felt better, had a sense of direction finally. He put on his coat to leave. Klaussen. He really should give the man a call. The diary might be fun to read. He started around his desk for the phone, but thought, no, there's no hurry. There's really nothing startling to be found in Virginia. Detroit is where it's likely at. He decided Klaussen could wait a day. He wanted to go home and think. And then he wanted to talk to Darla.

Chapter 7

"Jesus, Grail, what *do* you know about your father?" Darla plopped alongside him on the sofa in Grail's study. "How can there be no photographs of him?"

Grail shrugged. "Mom said he didn't like having his picture made. Indians used to resist that, too. They believed it robbed them of their souls, I think."

"Forget the Indians. You're telling me there's no baby pictures, no high school graduation stuff—no nothing?"

"Nothing. Nada. My father's family pictures were destroyed in a fire."

"That's weird enough to be from some made for TV movie," Darla said.

"I know. It's as though he was a spy, a man without a country—without an identity."

Darla frowned. "So, Hudson, how *do* you picture your Dad?"

"An empty frame." Grail opened the two Bell's beers he had fetched from the refrigerator and handed her one. "Of course, I could always go to Wal-Mart and buy one of those frames that already has someone's picture in it."

"How bizarre," she said. "You could throw a party and introduce everyone to your dad from Wal-Mart." She drank a large gulp.

"How about this," Grail said. "I put a picture of Robert Redford on the mantle and see if anyone notices."

"They'd notice, Hudson, and you don't have a mantle. Just a fireplace."

"We can probably get a mantle at Wal-Mart."

"That's the spirit," she said. "Positive thinking." She leaned closer to Grail and slipped an arm around his shoulders.

"Are you always going to call me Hudson?" he said.

"Yes. Unless I'm mad at you, and then I'll call you Grail. Now you'll always know when I'm mad."

"Will you be mad at me very often?"

"I don't know. I don't think so."

They kissed, a hungry, lingering kiss.

"Keep kissing like that and I'll never get mad," she said. "But what about you? Will you get mad at me like you get about your father?"

Grail pulled away slightly, felt surprise. "What makes you think I'm mad at my father?"

"I don't know—just the look on your face sometimes when you mention him." "What look?"

"Truthfully? It's sort of a mix of sadness and anger."

Grail got up off the sofa and walked over to the fireplace, thought better of it and returned. He slipped an arm around her waist. "He's been dead more than 40 years, Darla. And I never knew him. How can he make me angry?"

"Maybe you feel abandoned," she said. "Do you? I would."

This was something Grail had not thought of, but maybe it explained his dreams, the smoky presence of his father in those dreams. He had not told her yet of the dreams. He wasn't sure if he should tell her about Robert E. Lee in a g-string. That was just plain weird, no matter how much Richard Ewell had tried to explain it.

"Fess, up, Hudson. How do you feel about your father?" She got up before he could answer and headed toward the refrigerator. "I'll get us a couple more beers. Why don't we sit on the deck? Is that OK with you?"

"Yeah. But do I still have to spill my guts?"

"Of course," she called from the kitchen. "You have to tell me everything."

Darla brought tortilla chips and salsa with the beer. They sat at the table overlooking the garden. The sun was low and orange, without much heat but still full of light, and the beams filtered warmly through the cracks in the fence.

"I've always had my Mom," Grail said after a lengthy silence. "She's always been supportive. And growing up in Kalamazoo, my uncle Jack filled in for my dad as best he could. He took me to see the Tigers in Detroit, football games at Ann Arbor. Fatherly stuff."

"What was your Uncle Jack like?"

"He was a good guy. A decent man. He probably drank a little more than he should have, but it just made him sort of jolly. He even had values, I suppose. Maybe I got some of that from him. I don't think I turned out so bad, even though I never knew my dad."

A gray cat appeared. It had slipped through a wide crack in the fence and when it saw Grail it galloped to see him.

"This is Vernon," Grail said as he stroked behind the cat's ears and under his chin. "He lives next door but takes most of his meals over here."

"He knows where the kindhearted people live," Darla said. "More proof that you did turn out all right, Hudson."

"Think so?"

"Yeah," Darla said. "I think so. But it doesn't mean you don't have a need that wants to be filled."

Grail sipped his beer and admitted to himself she was probably right. Needs were always tough to figure. And it certainly had been the easy way out all these years to just sort of ignore him, to pretend he never really existed. For all practical purposes, Grail reminded himself, he really didn't exist. Well, it wasn't that simple.

"Do you think I need some sort of closure, Darla? Hell, maybe a good old exorcism for the troublesome spirit?"

She laughed. "Maybe an exorcism to set a good spirit free, not to get rid of a bad one. You're so dramatic, Hudson."

"I am not," he said, but knew he was and he forced a smile. "How would it be a good spirit and not a bad one? What do you mean?"

She sat her beer down. "I guess I mean, there's nothing to be gained by looking at him as bad, so let *your* spirit free. Be free of it all. Fill the need to move on, I guess. Be free, Hudson."

Free. The simplicity was surprising to Grail. A ceremony was in order. A freedom ceremony. Grail would get liberated. He needed it, he supposed. His father needed to be buried at last. Fully buried, with Grail liberated from the memory. There was no grave—another oddity he realized he had accepted awfully easily as a boy and had not questioned as a man. And so there was no place for mourning. Grail had been left only with the hope that his mother was right, that the soul of Lewis Hudson had been resurrected and rehabilitated from a watery grave like the sword Excalibur and flown north by God to the Hereafter.

"Earth to Hudson," Darla said. "You're haunted. We better do something about that before you turn into Hamlet and start talking to your dad's ghost."

Grail decided they should go to Kalamazoo for the weekend and forever banish his father's wandering soul to that mysterious land his mother called the kingdom of souls. They didn't yet know *how* this would be possible. That would have to come to them on the way to Michigan. All Grail knew for sure was that his father truly was a restless and wandering soul, even though he had never materialized in agony, because the body had never been recovered from Lake Erie and put properly to rest. Grail had already felt comfort of sorts in knowing the effort would be made.

But first they made satiny and lingering love until very early in the morning, and after dawn, when sparrows stirred in the pines outside the bedroom, not once did Grail confuse them with the haunting whispers of the soul of Lewis Hudson, although for the briefest of moments the thought did streak across his mind.

Chapter 8

▼

The City of New Orleans pitched and rolled through gentle curves splitting green cornfields on its way north from Champaign to Chicago. Darla napped and Grail kept track of the towns: Rantoul, Paxton, Onarga, Gilman, Kankakee, and then finally noisy Union Station, where they would catch the train to Kalamazoo in a few hours.

They caught a cab to the Water Tower on Michigan Avenue. The avenue was awash in a human sea of lawyers, accountants, and other business types too distracted, or perhaps too jaded by an obsession with wealth, to notice the majestic old tower. Grail stopped to study its ruddy gray features and that was when Darla revealed the tiny brass urn filled with sand.

"Jesus," Grail said. "That's supposed to be my dad? Where'd you get the sand?"

"True Value," she said. "The stuff isn't just lying around Champaign, you know."

"And the urn?"

"Walgreen's. Why can't it represent your dad, Grail?"

Grail held up the urn and examined it. He shook it and felt the sand shift. "No reason, I guess. It's kind of creepy." He handed it back to her. "But I'll play along, I guess."

"That's the spirit, Hudson. It's just a ceremony and the urn is just a symbol."

Grail smirked. "Right. OK, let's take dear old dad here and buy him lunch in a good place. From what Mom said, I'll bet he never had many meals in fancy restaurants."

They ate linguini and good California merlot behind the Water Tower at Bistro 25. Darla joked about not drinking too much wine: "Somebody has to be the designated urn carrier."

"We can get as hooched up as we want," Grail said. "We're going by train and cab."

"Are you going to get drunk, Hudson?"

"Maybe a little. Not much, I guess. Hell, this dead father ceremony still kind of spooks me some."

Darla sat the urn on the table to see what sort of rise she could get out of their snooty waiter, a thin and pale boy with a black turtleneck that seemed to come up over his chin. His lips twitched when Darla ordered three martinis.

"Three?"

"Yes, and a candle," Grail said. "You have candles, don't you?"

Darla arched her eyebrows.

"Three martinis, and a candle," the waiter said. "Are you expecting a third party?"

Grail pointed at the urn. "One's for him."

The waiter regarded the urn coolly, then looked at Grail. "Who is he?"

"My father. God rest his tormented soul."

"Oh, my," the waiter said. He retreated a step and then glanced around, as though looking for help.

"And the candle?" the waiter said.

"That's for him, too," Grail said.

"The candle signifies an anniversary?" the waiter asked.

"It sure does," Grail said. "It signifies his death. We've been waiting for the right time to honor him, and then bury him, of course."

"Of course," the waiter said quietly. "Which anniversary—how long, I mean."

"A little over forty years," Grail said.

"That's quite a wait," the waiter said.

"We're on our way to Michigan to bury the ashes," Darla said, unable to suppress a grin. "I'm sure you understand that it's a very solemn occasion."

"Yes," the waiter said, regaining some composure. "Three martinis and a candle. Coming right up. Oh, what color of candle?"

"What are the choices?" Darla said.

"Red, yellow, green, brown. Maybe blue."

Darla turned to Grail. "Wasn't red his favorite color?"

"Indeed it was," Grail said. "He loved red. He was passionate about anything red. Bring red. And plenty of olives in the drinks. My dad was a big olive man."

After their drinks Darla accidentally knocked over the urn and sand spilled on the table. The waiter walked by and his eyes got very big. He probably had never imagined human remains all over the fine lace tablecloth and he appeared petrified. He grabbed a napkin and butter knife but could not quite force himself into action.

"I certainly don't mean any disrespect," the waiter said.

"That's OK," Grail said. He scooped the sand into a neat little pile and scraped it off the edge of the table into a napkin. The waiter winced when Grail held it up and poured it back into the urn. Darla wouldn't look up for fear she would laugh. Grail was holding it back, too.

You know," the waiter said, "it looks remarkably like sand."

"Really?" Grail said. "That never occurred to me."

After lunch they headed south on Michigan Avenue, past Sak's and Eddie Bauer, and across a plaque on the street marking an old fort from the earliest days of the city. They strolled casually, holding hands, across the bridge spanning the Chicago River, which was green and foamy and topped with tour boats. Grail spotted the sign for the Billy Goat Tavern and wanted a drink so he could say he had been there, and then they hailed a cab back to Union Station and got on the Michigan train.

"There's Soldier Field," Darla said. "You can see it plain as day."

"The Bears are having a lousy year," Grail said. 'But the stadium looks nice. I love those columns."

"The poor Bears," Darla said. "How about your year, Hudson? Is it better than the Bears?"

"It's interesting so far. Time will tell." He was a little dopey from the alcohol.

Later Darla noticed the Calumet River. "We're making the curve to go up toMichigan."

"Good old Michigan," Grail said, yawning. 'I may take a nap on you."

She leaned into him and rested her head against his shoulder. He could smell her perfume. Here we are, he thought, two cats purring and fitting together nicely.

"I might take a little nap myself," Darla said.

"You're entitled."

"How's that?"

"You're the designated urn carrier. You did your duty while I hooched it up in the big city."

"Oh, yes," she said. "I protected the sacred family sand."

She did sleep, but Grail remained awake as the train lurched from stop to stop, but not unpleasantly, and with an ease and unobtrusiveness that made him think it could be any year in history. Any year at all, unless one looked out a window and saw the junk cars in the yards by the tracks, or the belching smokestacks of Gary, Indiana, where surely, Grail thought, the soil must be toxic. But it could be any time that train travel existed, and it could have been 1864, the time Grail sometimes understood better than any other, the days of the Civil War and especially the CSA, his specialty. Aided by the train's steady rocking and Darla tucked against him he transplanted himself through time and thought how easily they could be a couple on their way to Washington, DC, just as a Confederate Army under Jubal Early made its desperate bid to capture the Yankee capital and end a war that would create two countries.

Grail began to think, a half-dream, perhaps, that he lived in times too civilized, in a way, although how ironic to call it civilized as long as there was the Middle East and Oklahoma City and Bosnia, and a hundred other meat grinders. But here in the U.S., anyway—of the C.S.A. he could never quite be sure—life was all too placid an existence of modern conveniences and cell phones and deadlines, and the need to get rich, to be richer than the neighbors—to be the center of one's own movie and obsessed with style and not aware of the desperate fundamental need for substance.

He looked around: everyone is in a rush to get someplace—but where exactly? Getting ahead. Ahead? What does that mean exactly? Ahead of what? It was selfish, this notion of being ahead of something, someone. Competition, too—the foundation plank of capitalism—that's about getting ahead. It's about beating the other guy to the riches. How was that civilized? It's tribal, Grail knew. It's what they practiced in prehistoric times and now it has been refined into art and science. How can it be civilized for teenagers to be consumed by cell phones and pagers and Tommy Hilfiger clothes and Michael Jordan shoes they literally will kill for? People should ride a train. Yes, that was the beginning of the answer. They should ride a train and allow themselves to be swept along elegantly and slowly, with time to look out a window and watch barrel-chested civilization rush past in a hurry to go in a circle.

Darla woke up as they passed through the station at Niles, Michigan. She didn't speak and instead just smiled sleepily up at Grail. They looked out the window at thick woods and more sleepy little towns and then they were in Kalamazoo in a rental car on the way to Milham Park, which was on the way to the house where Grail's mother lived.

At the park Grail guided Darla to a shallow stream infested with ducks and geese looking for handouts from parents herding children.

"I guess this is the place," Grail said. "He died in water and so we return him to water. There's a pond on the other side of the park if you think that's better."

"This is perfect, Hudson. The pond would be too slow. This stream is alive."

"With ducks," Grail said, and several sailed over to the bank where he stood. "Sorry, I have nothing for you today—just sand."

"Don't think of it as sand," Darla said. She handed Grail the urn. "It symbolizes your father. Try and let it set you both free."

"This will make us free?"

"If you let it. It's in your power to make it happen."

Grail emptied the urn in the clear, shallow water and watched the sand drift and then settle to the pebbly bottom. That was that. It was over in an instant. More ducks and geese arrived and kept up a steady racket. Several more swam over to the shore, and one goose eyed Grail intently.

"What if my father was reincarnated as a goose? That could be him."

"Well, then you'll look mighty funny trying to hug that goose."

The goose swam away, honking loudly. Grail wasn't sure a hug was what he would want.

"Do you feel differently?" Darla asked. "Do you feel good?"

"I don't know." They walked back to their car. "Do you suppose it should have a delayed effect?"

"Maybe. Give it time."

"Sure," Grail said. "That's what I'll do. Maybe it's like drugs, and it kicks in later. Are you ready to go meet my Mom?"

"I think so. Sure—of course."

"Really?"

"Really, Hudson. Now, what are we going to do with this urn?"

Chapter 9

▼

Grail's mother was pruning bushes in front of her house with a large pair of shears when Grail and Darla pulled into the driveway. She put the shears on a window ledge and smoothed her dress firmly before striding briskly toward the car. A sudden breeze made wings out of her straight red hair.

She's always been sort of a determined woman, Grail thought as he got out and smiled at his mother. He wondered how his father must have fared with her determination, and he figured this visit was maybe a good chance to look into that some. They hugged and then Lorraine took a long look at Darla.

"Awfully pretty," she concluded. "Hi, I'm Lorraine."

Darla took Lorraine's hand. It was warm and the grip solid. "I'm so happy to meet you, Mrs. Hudson."

"Please, call me Lorraine. I hear Mrs. Hudson all day at school. How was your trip?"

"It was good," Darla said. "We had lunch in Chicago and saw some of the city."

"How nice," Lorraine said. "There's not so much to see around here, but it's a nice enough town. Is this your first time in Kalamazoo? Grail said on the phone you're from Michigan."

"I'm from Mt. Pleasant. I visited Kalamazoo a few times when I was little. We used to have cousins down here, but they're mostly scattered now."

"I almost went to Mt. Pleasant for graduate school," Lorraine said. "But I ended up in Ann Arbor instead. How do you like it down at Illinois?"

"I like the school," Darla said. "The town is a little backward sometimes."

"Too many Republicans," Lorraine said. "We have that problem here, too."

They laughed and Grail felt unexpectedly juvenile, as though he was there to offer his prom date for inspection and it was he who was failing.

"So, Mom, how's the old house holding up?" He gave it a quick look. It always looked neat and solid, just like his mother.

"The house is holding up pretty well," Lorraine said.

"I see that," Grail said. "You look good, too."

"I stay busy. School and the house keep me going. That's the secret to life, if there is one. Bring your stuff in and we'll go out back and sit on the patio. I made some fresh iced tea."

Darla followed Lorraine inside while Grail fetched their bags from the car. He was happy to be home, even if just for a couple days. It had been more than a year. He sat the bags on the sidewalk and took a closer look at the house, a lovely old Tudor well-shaded by oaks. He'd made a tree house in one of them a very long time ago, but he could still see the scars where it had been nailed to limbs. He looked fondly at the roof where it sloped down over his bedroom, where in the winters he and Frankie Carlyle from down the street used to slide off into the snow banks driven high against the house. Grail wondered whatever happened to Frankie. Did he ever come home and stare at his old house and remember all the little things? Grail knew that many people visited the houses they grew up in and thought they had shrunk over time, but as he lumbered through the front door he didn't feel that way at all.

The talk turned to reunification over dinner. When Grail announced he would soon go to the C.S.A. to observe and gather material for a book, Lorraine seemed to have expected that; but Grail noticed she grew a little pensive and he could not understand why. She finally wished him much luck and even proposed a toast. They drank several and it made them all jolly for a while, but during dessert Darla let is slip about the urn filled with sand and Milham Park and Lorraine was visibly disturbed by it.

No one spoke as Lorraine cleared the table and put the dishes in the dishwasher. Darla helped, but Grail couldn't find anything meaningful to do. He hovered awkwardly before settling against a counter.

"It was just a thing to do symbolically," Grail finally said, and he thought his voice sounded louder than it should.

"I quite understand that part of it," Lorraine said. She wiped her hands on a kitchen towel and then carefully folded it and draped it over the faucet.

"It was my idea, Mrs. Hudson—Lorraine," Darla said. "I hope I haven't offended you."

Lorraine met Darla's gaze. "No, child, you haven't offended me. It just surprised me." She fiddled with the towel and faucet. "Let me get used to it. Who would like coffee?"

Darla looked around and spotted the coffeemaker. "Please, Lorraine, let me do that. I make pretty good coffee."

"She does," Grail said, almost happy just to have something to say.

"That would be fine," Lorraine said.

"You two go out to the living room and I'll bring it when it's ready," Darla said. She sensed Lorraine had more to say to Grail. After they left Darla found the bathroom around the corner from the kitchen and brushed her hair and splashed cold water on her face. She took her time and then went back to the kitchen and made the coffee, resisting the urge to try and listen through the kitchen door. Once she was sure she heard Grail's voice, but she could not make out the words.

Darla poked around the kitchen and discovered a silver serving tray and matching cups and saucers with an H for Hudson on them. When she served the coffee she thought Grail looked agitated but was trying to hide it. Lorraine seemed very grim and tired. They all drank their coffee quietly, like strangers in a diner. Grail smiled at Darla once, weakly, and raised his eyebrows.

"Are you tired," he asked Darla, and she knew it was a cue. She finished her coffee and excused herself to go upstairs to bed. She knew that whatever was happening between Grail and Lorraine needed to unfold some more.

It was more than an hour before Grail went upstairs. He slipped off his clothes and pulled on pajama bottoms. Darla pretended to be asleep. She felt him sit on the edge of the bed. After a while she figured he needed to talk and she was thankful for it. She reached an arm out and slid it around his waist.

"You two talked so long," Darla said. "Does that mean it's a doozy?"

Grail turned and smirked slightly. "Oh, yeah. It's a doozy alright." He shook his head.

"Was she really that freaked by the ceremony?" Darla said.

Grail chuckled nervously. "Nope. In fact, after a bit she concluded it made sense from my perspective."

"Really?" Darla felt better.

"That's right," Grail said.

"Really?" Darla said. "She said that?"

"She did."

"Well, what was the past hour about? Did it take that long just for her to get over it?"

"No, that part went by pretty fast." Grail was remembering it and shaking his head again. "We were getting past it when you brought out the coffee."

"God, Hudson—you and your mom were like the walking dead."

Grail looked at her. "Apparently we're not the only ones."

"What does that mean?"

"It means we sure as hell performed the wrong ceremony at the park." He had a glazed look. "Because my father isn't dead after all." He ran a hand through his hair.

"No way. He's alive?"

"Yeah, he's alive. How about that shit." He looked away. "*That's* why she was so freaked at dinner. That's what we were talking about for so long."

"Good God, Hudson. But she told you he was dead. This is too weird. All these years you thought he died while you—"

"While I was still in the womb. Yeah, I was told he drowned in Lake Erie. Now I know it was just a cover story."

Darla sat up. "Jesus H. Christ. Why the big fricking secret?"

Grail said nothing for a long moment, then shrugged. "To protect me, I guess. I'm not even born yet and already they're divorced, and so maybe she thought it would help. She maybe thought she was protecting me. She was young. Later maybe she was afraid I would want to go find him when I was growing up. She sure as hell doesn't think much of him. She divorced him and made him agree to disappear from my life. He went along ith it."

Darla put both arms around him. Her naked breasts rubbed his back and she kissed his neck. "Are you OK? I know that's a dumb question."

"It's not so dumb." He reached behind him to hug her waist. "I'll be fine. It's not like I know the guy. I don't have anything invested in it." He didn't know yet whether he really believed that. He wanted to believe that.

"It's not that simple," she said. "You think it is, but it's not." She kissed his neck some more.

"I suppose," he said. "But I don't know the guy. That makes a huge difference."

"Maybe. Jesus, Hudson, I don't know what to say. Are you mad at Lorraine?"

He thought about that. Was he? He didn't think so. He couldn't be sure. He tried to look at it intellectually: his mom wanted to protect him. From what? She said he—his father—had turned out to be a "southern radical." He "spouted venom about the U.S.A. and the idea that the two countries could ever reunite. Spouted venom? That didn't sound like his mother. Well, he guessed there likely was much he didn't know about his mother. Anyway, she didn't discover until after they were married that he—Lewis Hudson—was also a womanizer. Getting married had been an impetuous decision. She didn't know him well enough, but he had been handsome and charming. She was a girl then. Not much more than a girl. A college girl. Lewis Hudson was a foreigner with a "delicious way of speaking." So, she was seduced. She had learned from that. End of story. For her, maybe.

"No, I don't think I'm mad at her," he said. "It wouldn't help things. She did what she thought was best at the time."

"I know," Darla said. "But she might have told you before now."

"Yes," he said after a moment. "I think she should have."

"So, Hudson—where does this dweeby father of yours live?"

"In the C.S.A. Maryland. Not far from D.C."

"You'll be there soon."

"I will."

"It'll be some damn adventure."

"How do you mean?" Grail frowned.

"I mean, you'll go find him—won't you?"

Grail found that hard to visualize. "I don't know. Maybe he's not easy to find. I wouldn't even know where to look."

"Did your mom give any clues as to where he might be?"

"I suppose." He tried hard to remember specific details. "Yeah, she mentioned some places. But it's not automatic I look for him."

"Isn't it, Hudson."

That was the question Grail took with him when he finally slept. It was the question on his mind all the next day when they took the train back to Illinois.

Part II

Chapter 10

Mallory Hampton Wade III, scion of an old and illustrious Virginia family, summa cum laude from Vanderbilt, descendant of colonels and majors and captains who gloriously served and died for The Cause, secret admirer of the wit of Abraham Lincoln, owner of a cheap Dali but a pricey Picasso, advocate of *Saving Private Ryan* over *Shakespeare in Love* as best picture, lover of Jane Austen and not Tama Janowitz, was quietly but nonetheless heartily masturbating.

It was morning and one of the rare cool days before summer kicked in with a humid vengeance. Wade was committing the forbidden act—alleviating stress was his euphemism for it—while sitting at his antique desk, which had been used briefly at Gettysburg—but certainly not for masturbation—by Longstreet, who though it too dainty. The desk suited Wade, who was short and who would have been considered smallish except that he had a tendency, thanks to excellent California cabernets he acquired regularly (bribes) through the trade department, to allow his gut to become a rubbery roof for his belt buckle.

But he was being most careful and as silent as could be, and the tapping noise a knuckle sometimes made on the upstroke when it struck the desk ever so gently, was even less than the sharp low strike of a typewriter key. He had to be especially careful, because Mrs. Fines—Amanda Danforth Fines, of the South Carolina Fines—had the annoying habit of just bursting in unannounced. Wade had told her countless times to knock; after all, he was a C.S.A. assistant protocol secretary of state with a lavish office at P.G.T, Beauregard Plaza, in the Jefferson Davis State Department Building; and it was a job, by God and General Lee, that had cost his daddy, the right honorable Mr. MalloryHampton Wade II, considerable cajoling and howling at the elbow of President Carter, a suspect Georgian, when

Carter wasn't sure he had the voters of the glorious state of Virginia in his hip pocket. Virginia, by God and General Lee, was sacred Wade territory.

Mrs. Fine was Wade's personal assistant, and she didn't seem ever to be impressed by the Wade family money, which officially was made in shipping but actually got its greatest boost from bootlegging bourbon up to the Yankee cities after the Great Patriotic War reached its glorious conclusion. She certainly never appeared much impressed by Wade III's status in the department. She talked to him sometimes as though she was his nanny and he a great unkempt and naughty boy with too much time on his hands. Or, as in this particular moment, too much of his own flesh in his hands.

Wade knew he should have just locked the door; but a locked door always suggested shenanigans, and actually, Wade had discovered he liked the risk involved with an unlocked door; not that he wanted to get caught. Heavens, no. Being unmasked as a tosser, as the English say, at State would surely earn the perpetrator an assignment in some dank region—the Middle East, perhaps—where jerkoff jockeys probably got their hand and offending member chopped off.

Undaunted, Wade went at his task—the five-digit dialysis, he called it—with practiced efficiency and began to relax. The stress was really going away and the world seemed almost divine again. He kept up a nice rhythm and found himself oddly thinking of his wife, Arlene, which surprised him. Usually he thought of that sexy Miss Grimes down the hall in the computer services office who wore short skirts and bent over a lot.

Besides, how bad was it really? Hadn't Hemingway joked about it in A Farewell to Arms? Sure. Absolutely. It was perhaps Wade's favorite novel and he had read it as a kid, a few years before the cultural ban on Yankee literature had been lifted. A copy had been smuggled in through Wade family connections, of which there were many, and Wade understood immediately when the priest, Frederick Henry's friend, was being teased by soldiers who said he was "five against one." Well, Wade was five against one big time now, and then it was over just as the door did creak open, Mrs. Fine cruising in with a stack of papers and a stern downward glance. Wade, ever the contingency man, was ready for her: he slid smoothly forward in his chair, the offending lap and open fly tucked under the desk, and with satiny aplomb—even a subtle flourish of the fingers—folded both stubby, pink hands on his desk, assuming just as stern a look as the one worn by Mrs. Fine.

"The secretary sent down some more visa applications," Mrs. Fine said, referring to C.S.A. State Secretary Titus La Grange Finch. "I reckon they're the last batch before reunification makes them obsolete."

"Yes, Mrs. Fine. Indeed. Well, then things will be quite well in hand," Wade said, enjoying the daring of his joke. Then he remembered that his fly was down and his smile tumbled off his ample cheeks. Mrs. Fine noticed his distress and raised her eyebrows.

"Is everything OK, Mr. Wade? You look a little flush. I declare, your cheeks make me think of cranberries."

Wade almost said he had a good grip on things, but realized it was time to shift back to the reality of State. He zipped his fly after Mrs. Fines put the stack of papers on his desk and turned away to open a file cabinet.

"I'm doing well, Mrs. Fines. I'm not sure why you saw those cranberries."

"Why, your checks were red," she said over her shoulder. "Maybe it's the cool weather. It sure is unusual for this time of year."

"Here in Virginia we call it the Lee Breeze," Wade said as he stood and smoothed his pleated dark trousers, checking quickly to make sure there was no telltale bulge. "You've heard of the Lee Breeze down in South Carolina, haven't you Mrs. Fines?"

Mrs. Fines glanced out the window and saw the branches of an elm ruffled by gentle breezes. Wade studied her: she was 45 and leaning toward dowdiness, but still had firm breasts and shapely, long legs, and her blonde hair, which fell on her shoulders, framed her face sweetly. He suppressed the thought for fear of jump-starting the old erector set.

"Surely," Mrs. Fines said. "But in South Carolina, of course, it's referred to as Longstreet's Breeze."

"Yes, of course," Wade said, quickly rolling his eyes. Mrs. Fines had lived in the capital for nearly ten years but still thought of herself as a South Carolinian. She was also a member of, but perhaps not rabidly so, the sect of revisionists who had re-evaluated Lee and judged him human and error-prone at Gettysburg when he ignored Longstreet's pleas to hook to the right and flank Meade's army. Lee was an icon in Virginia, but just a statue to people such as Mrs. Fines. Wade had heard her tell Mrs. Grimes and others how Lee must have been giddy or dumbstruck or just plain stupid at Gettysburg for not seeing what Longstreet had repeatedly pointed out, that for a time there was a clear path to the right of those two little hills that might have enabled Lee's army to roll up the unsuspecting Federals: and of course, that would have made the valiant but bloody stupid slaughter of Pickett's Charge unnecessary. Mrs. Fines had studied history at the University of South Carolina and was confident in the knowledge. Wade often found history tedious. We live *now*, he said to himself.

"But I'll grant you we have more humidity in South Carolina, "Mrs. Fines said suddenly, as though coming back from a daydream and remembering they were conversing. She gathered the papers in Wade's out box and hurried out the door with the same stern, downward glance she had when she came in.

Wade went to the window and looked out at the Potomac. The grand old river had nearly been re-named after the war, it being the name of Grant's army, of course, but there was sentiment for keeping natural things the way they had always been. Lee himself, who lived on its banks after the war, said he didn't know if he could get used to calling the river by any other name, and Lee's wishes became the C.S.A.'s imperatives.

A yacht cruised by, its bow wave foamy and white, the stars and bars fluttering in Lee's Breeze. So much history had flowed with that river, Wade thought. He knew his history as well as Mrs. Fines. Better. After all, he was a Vandy graduate. With honors. Mrs. Fines had not finished her senior year at South Carolina because she got married to Mr. Fines, an obscure commerce department official, and moved to D.C. But history sure seemed to suit Mrs. Fines more than it did Wade, who was in a hurry to discover the future after reunification. His future.

By late afternoon Wade had reviewed all but two of the visa applications. The two most troublesome ones. One was a request from the infamous porn star Robert Whitfield, a.k.a. Wad Upshot, whose most prominent film surely was "The South Will Rise Again." Wade had seen that one, and indeed Wad Upshot rose again and again, and again, but it wasn't what the factions opposed to reunification had in mind when they coined the phrase and voiced their feelings that reunification was defeat after all.

Upshot, a Virginian, wanted to visit his dying brother, but his "profession" had hung (Wade smirked at the word) up his application, and now it was up to Wade to advise his boss, Secretary Finch, on whether to let Upshot into the country. On the one hand (another smirk) to deny him was in keeping with the morality imperatives of the C.S.A. But to let him visit his brother had its advantages: it might impress the United States by showing compassion and help smooth along reunification. Upshot's dear mother in Alexandria had spoken out on television on her stud son's behalf. It seemed that even porn stars could do no wrong in the eyes of their mothers. Wade was grateful that Mrs. Whitfield didn't call him Wad and instead used the endearing "Bobby." That image of the wayward son needing an opportunity to change could be useful if State decided to let Upshot in. Pornography was a fact of life in the C.S.A. Wade had even heard some of the office girls discussing Upshot's "qualifications." Several laughingly offered to "sponsor" him as a C.S.A. guest. But porn wasn't the thriving industry like in the U.S. and the decision required some thought.

Wade decided to ponder the Upshot dilemma a while and moved on to case number two: Grail Hudson, the prominent University of Illinois historian and sometimes critic of the C.S.A. He had read Hudson's book, which had been banned for a time, and enjoyed the sections on Lincoln's sense of humor. Hudson was asking to visit so he could witness the reunification process. No doubt he would write another book, or at the very least, articles in prominent Yankee magazines, such as the Atlantic and New Yorker. His opinion carried some weight and he could become either an asset to reunification or the fly in the ointment. Banning Hudson clearly seemed to Wade a decision that would invite grumbling from the Yankees, perhaps causing grief for Finch, and grief had a habit of rolling downhill. Then again, the Yankees weren't likely to withdraw from reunification, the thing they so desperately wanted and thousands died for, over the ruffled feathers of a prairie academic.

Wade decided to recommend admitting Hudson, and as for Upshot, he'd throw the subject on the table with Finch and see what the boss thought. Having set a course, Wade felt happy. He eased back in his chair and watched out the window. He would go see Finch soon, but not right away. Life worked best when taken slowly and deliberately, he decided. That was the C.S.A. way. It was a lesson the Yankees could use, Wade thought, but no, they were usually in a rush to do something, to invent something, build a huge industry, spread capitalism without regard for consequences. Wade swung his legs up on to his desk and clasped his hand behind his head. The window really made all the difference in his office. As he gazed out over the Potomac, it began to rain and the yacht had re-appeared, struggling now to head upriver. Its Confederate battle flag was drenched and limp, and Wade could see a man in the wheelhouse lean out the window to try and see where he was going.

Finch's door was open and Wade entered gingerly. Finch the Grinch's moods were a tad upredictable, but the open door was a good sign. Still, Wade made sure to rap his knuckles a couple times firmly on the door just in case. Finch had his back to Wade and was looking out his window at the Potomac, his hands clasped behind him. Finch was tall and slim, a stately figure, and when he turned around Wade was relieved to see that he was smiling.

"Ah, Wade. Yes, do come in, my boy. I was going to send for you. You must be a mind reader."

"Just your humble servant," Wade said, a little too smarmily, but Finch didn't seem to notice. Finch maneuvered Wade to a chair and then folded his imposing frame into his custom-made, padded, high-backed chair behind the massive oak desk. There were dozens of photographs on it. Some were family, but many were the rich and famous and very powerful that Finch had hobnobbed with, and who had greased the way for the ascension to his current lofty position. There were several pictures of him with President Carter as they nailed a roof for Habitat for Humanity, a chore Finch privately disliked but publicly praised. Carter did not know that, of course. Finch also loved the glitz and glow that came with celebrities and there was a cluster of pictures of him with actors: Harrison Ford, Clint Eastwood, and of course, John Wayne. The Wayne photo had been taken aboard the star's converted minesweeper moored near the Fort Sumter Memorial. Finch was reportedly among the very last people to speak with Wayne before the actor died of cancer.

There was an awkward silence. There was always an awkward silence. Wade knew that anyone visiting Finch the Grinch had to fidget a moment or two before the great man spoke. Wade was never sure if Finch needed a moment to collect his thoughts or if the man used it to humble visitors. The silence did tend to force people's eyes upon the dazzling array of photographs positioned so guests would know who was in them, and of course one couldn't fail to notice the Rembrandt that hung behind the desk. President Carter had visited the office once and like the lowliest protocol secretary had to content himself with picking lint from his trousers while Finch rediscovered the ability to speak. Afterwards Carter told an aide that there was something difficult to articulate but very palpable in the atmosphere of Finch's domain that seemed to compel people—even presidents—to let Finch speak first.

"Wade," Finch said, and then his voice trailed off as he again gazed out the window momentarily.

"Yes, sir?" Wade studied Finch's impassive face. The man was nearly 70 but still handsome. It was the tan, Wade decided, that made him look younger and that made him fit in so well with the actors and other celebrities whose company he relished.

"Wade, what do you think of this professor Hudson?" I mean as a man."

There was another awkward silence, this time generated by Wade, who hadn't thought about Hudson beyond whether it would be advantageous or not to allow him into the country. The truth was, Wade didn't really know what sort of man Hudson was beyond what Hudson had written in his book, *Birth of a Rebel Nation*.

Wade adjusted the knot of his tie, then cleared his throat. "He's no friend of Robert E. Lee, that's for sure. He makes it clear enough in the book. You've read it, sir?"

"Yes." Finch's lips pursed slightly and Wade knew the question was stupid. Not much escaped Finch, who had been a professor of political science at The University of Virginia.

"Well, sir, then you know the man practically accuses Lee of hating blacks even though he opposed slavery."

"Old news. Lee was Lee and made some statements perhaps best forgotten. What else?"

"He's from Michigan, and quite proud of it. He was born in the same town associated with Custer. Monroe, Michigan. It's south of Detroit."

"Is that significant to you?"

"It's bedrock Yankee country. I take it to mean he's a staunch Union man."

"Yes, "Finch said. "No doubt. Do you think he's one of those who don't want reunification?"

"I don't know, sir. What would be his motivation for that?"

Revenge, Wade. Revenge is the oldest and best motivation of all. You said yourself he's a staunch Union man, but the Union was denied—has been denied, perhaps in his view, for these 135 years. Maybe he doesn't want us back."

"I guess I don't see what's to be gained by that view, sir. He can't stop reunification."

"No, he can't, "Finch said "But he could light a fire under the anti-Union faction. I'm not saying he will. I just want to know if it's feasible.

"I would say it's not likely, sir. My take on Hudson is that he sells more copies of his book by taking potshots at us."

"Yes, a little hand-wringing and venom is usually good for that. So, Wade, do we let him in? Shall we grant him access to reunification backstage?"

"With proper supervision, yes. He has influence. People will read him. We might make him useful to the process if he enjoys his time here."

"Excellent. My view exactly, and you've named your poison. I want you to supervise our Prof. Hudson, Wade. Perhaps chaperone is a better description. Regardless, I want you to convert him to our side. I want a smooth reunification. Carter wants a smooth reunification. See to it that Hudson is an asset in that regard, not a liability."

Wade sensed he had been dismissed, given his marching orders. He was a little stunned by the assignment, but didn't dare show it to Finch. He rose and Finch offered a hand, which struck Wade as out of character but welcome nonetheless.

"I'll do my best, sir."

Chapter 11

▼

Rain lashed Grail's plane as it skimmed precariously low over the Potomac like a huge metal goose looking for a place to splash down. He could make out a few crimson motorboats dashing for shore, and the ghostly outlines of Georgetown University oozing out of the mist as the engines were throttled back some more. Jefferson Davis Island would appear under the wing in a few seconds, with just the George Pickett and J.E.B. Stuart bridges next before the Dixie Airways Boeing 727 banked gently to the right for final approach to Robert E. Lee National Airport on the Virginia side of the river.

Grail glanced across the aisle as the plane banked and saw Arlington below, the Lee Monument consumed by mist except for the pointed top, which suggested a white marble pyramid struggling futilely to escape gravity. The rain was unusual for this time of year and had been going on with few breaks for several weeks. The Potomac had leapt from its banks several times, and so much water had naturally raised the cherry tree-lined Tidal Basin and Washington Channel until they, too, had saturated streets and the low park south of the White House where the CSA had erected a controversial wall, designed by a Vietnamese woman, to honor its dead in Vietnam. President Carter had joked that it might be faster to get to Lee National by boat rather than car, to which his critics agreed but counseled him not to slow down should he choose that method of transportation because one never knew when another killer bunny might be lurking.

As soggy houses dripped out of the mist, the 727 abruptly clawed for altitude and circled the city in a holding pattern not expected to last more than twenty minutes, according to the flight attendant with sparkling stars and bars earrings. Hudson picked up the *New York Times* he had bought at JFK but forgot to read.

He was startled to read that a bomb had gone off the previous night in front of the United States embassy near DuPont Circle. No one had been injured, but to Hudson it was very chilling and reminiscent of IRA bombings in Ireland and England.

Would it come to terrorism? That had never occurred to him. Could a new, more deadly Civil War, one fueled by modern weaponry and even the threat of nuclear weapons, suddenly ignite and make the original conflict seem like a bar fight? He concluded that it wasn't possible. To think otherwise struck him as too much to bear. It just couldn't happen between two countries with 135 years of peace along their borders, two countries that had marched hand in hand, if not always flag in flag, through two world wars, Korea, and Vietnam, not to mention that pathetic little overkill that Reagan committed in the Caribbean.

But there omnipresent was the glaring example of England and Ireland, that perpetual violent madness between people that otherwise should know better. What was that about? Religion? No, that's too simple, he realized. It's religion and it's also about England not having the sense to realize it isn't the 1800s anymore; but it was also about religion in a pretty big way and Hudson found that hugely unfathomable. To kill others because of differences in worship. Wasn't it fundamentally the same God? Well, maybe not. But it wasn't as though it was the difference between Catholics and, say, the goofy Scientologists, or the greedy, misogynist Mormons, was it? In Ireland there was no goofy John Travolta, believing, apparently, that an alien race from some Star Wars-like place far, far away deposited humans on earth for whatever reasons that made Travolta happy. So, where did the humans come from? Why hadn't those vaunted spacemen, who Travolta had embarrassingly portrayed in a film, just exterminated humans a la Hitler's SS? Another story.

And the conflict between Ireland and England was also about murder. All conflicts, Hudson the historian and examiner of humanity, had long ago realized, elevated otherwise ordinary people to the status of murderers. How else could one explain a good deal of the Middle East, or the Balkans? Sure, there were very real issues there; at least at some point in history, but after a while it was just the cycle of hate and stupidity and conditioning that had taken over, and that was why Palestinians and Israelis kill each other, why Serbs and Croats brutalize women and children as easily as men, why the IRA can't give up it's guns and militancy. Because it likes it. It needs it. They all need and want and cherish the blood and it's what keeps them going. They can't accept being ordinary people, and so they don't. The modern malaise: the need to be epic. Was television, then, with its creation, illumination, and perpetuation of celebrity, the root cause of the world's problems? Yet another story.

Hudson rose a little from his seat to survey the other passengers, people he had not really thought much about when he boarded at JFK after a briefing by the U.S. State Department on what to expect in the C.S.A., and, perhaps, what they might expect in return as impressions of reunification from the other side. He looked up and down the aisle but could see little of what was there: men in Armani and men in polyester off the rack from Sears. Some were adulterers and some were not, and the cut of the cloth wasn't necessarily a clue. There were women in voluminous sun dresses and women in the trim navy blue corporate business uniform that revealed every curve, regardless of whether it was a good idea or not. A sprinkling of children fidgeted and leaped in their seats and pointed at everything. A gaggle of flight attendants cruised up and down the aisles with frozen smiles and their contempt held in check with great practice. Even one of the pilots, lanky and self-confident, had strolled through the cabin imperiously, assuring eager passengers that the flight was on time, but he was, Hudson figured, just in dire need of a bathroom.

How many of these people could become murderers? How many already were? Probably none at all. But once that was true in Ireland and the Balkans and the Middle East; and now a bomb had been used in the C.S.A., crossing a new threshold, creating a new dimension for the argument against reunification, giving birth to a new level for people to disagree on.

An attractive young woman across the aisle leaned over and studied the front page of the *Times* after Hudson picked it up and held it open in front of him. He could feel her eyes boring through the paper. He lowered the paper just enough to make eye contact and she smiled.

"I'm afraid I'm guilty of trying to read your paper. I hope that sort of thing doesn't annoy you."

Hudson smiled back. "That's OK. I catch myself doing it on planes, too."

The woman had short brown hair that framed her thin but pretty face very well, and her green eyes reminded Hudson of Darla. She was a little dark-skinned, a good tan, perhaps, and could have been of Italian descent, or maybe Hispanic.

"I was reading the bomb story," she said. "Such a terrible thing. The embassy staff sent me word of it last night in New York when I got back to my hotel, but the information was kind of sketchy. I see that no one was killed, thank God."

"Yeah. I was just thinking how it reminded me of the IRA."

"Oh, God, not that," she said. "Not here. I really hope it isn't coming to that. Maybe it was just a nut looking for attention."

"I hope you're right, but I guess I'm a pessimist when it comes to this sort of thing. I tend to assume the worst. Listen, I don't mean to pry, but were you referring to the C.S.A. embassy in New York? Are you with the government?"

"The State Department," she said. "I was in New York meeting with the U.S. state people. We're smoothing the way for talks, although this bomb thing makes me think that could get complicated. I'm Leslie Sheridan." She offered her hand and Hudson shook it. Her touch was warm and pleasant, and as they leaned toward each other he caught the tart scent of lemons.

"I'm Grail Hudson. Very nice to meet you."

"*Doctor* Grail Hudson? The professor from Illinois?" Their hands were still joined.

"Yes, have we met? I should be shot for not remembering if we have."

"No, we've never met. I have read your book, though. Most C.S.A. state department people have. Well, I can't know for sure if most have, but a lot. It's not required reading, but maybe it should be." Her smile was still there, but there was also a subtle hint of reproach. She carefully released his hand. Grail sensed her discomfort.

"The book. Well, I guess you're reconsidering that option of having me shot."

"A simple flogging would do nicely, Dr. Hudson," but she was still smiling.

"Please, call me Grail. If you're going to flog me, then we ought to be on a first name basis, don't you think?"

"I can't actually flog you, which is a pity, even though you've mangled the reputation of Robert E. Lee, the father of our country, the greatest gentleman and general that ever lived," She said tongue in cheek, but then quickly looked around to see if anyone had been listening.

"That Lee business will be the only thing people remember when I'm gone," he said, shaking his head. "All I did was draw attention to some post-war letters and let Lee's comments do the talking, but some people will never forgive me. How about you, Leslie? Will *you* forgive me?"

"Of course not. Never." She patted his knee. "I'm kidding. It's just the zealots who take that stuff seriously down here, and most of them are idiot windbags, like Rush Limbaugh. I guess it's not much different than being in a bar in Chicago or Minneapolis and saying Nixon was a crook who tried to subvert democracy, or Reagan was a senile old actor who stole from the poor and gave to the rich."

"That's priceless," Hudson said, laughing. "Somehow I have to work that into an article."

"Or your next book. See? You Yankees have had your share of scoundrels. Sort of puts it into perspective when this stuff about Lee comes up, doesn't it?"

"Point well taken. And it was a long time ago, I suppose. How about I make amends on this by buying you a drink—if this plane ever lands."

"I don't know, Grail. Can I be seen drinking with such a Lee hater?" and for a moment she wondered if it was, after all, a dangerous thing to do. But she found Hudson interesting and attractive, and he was a guest in her country.

"You'd be doing me a huge favor, I think," he said. "Your state folks are sending out some blueblood bloodhound to meet me. We could give him the slip."

"Blueblood bloodhound? Now there's a unique phrase. What do you mean?"

The name of my C.S.A. chaperone—I assume I'm going to be chaperoned because I'm such a well-known Lee hater—is Mallory Hampton Wade III. The name makes me think of some guy in silk underwear with his pudgy pinky finger permanently in the air."

"I know Mal Wade," she said, surprised. "*That's* who they're sending?"

"I got a letter from him just the other day. A regal production welcoming me to the C.S.A. and offering his services for exploring the many cultural avenues available in the capital—diplomat speak for watching my every move so I don't get into trouble, or find out something I shouldn't know."

"Well, Mal is pretty close to Finch, so I guess it makes sense after all. He'd make a good tour guide. Can't tell you if he wears silk undies, but, yeah, he's a blueblood alright. A Virginia blueblood."

"His name is interesting," Hudson said. "There was a Confederate general named Wade Hampton. A cavalry officer. This Mallory guy is Hampton Wade, just the reverse."

"Sorry, but I don't know the story on that," she said. "Knowing the Wade family, I'm sure it's complicated. Maybe even sordid."

"I can imagine," said Hudson, feeling the plane finally descending again. The Potomac reappeared and then the Virginia shore. Hudson could see the windshield wipers wiping on cars along the Jefferson Davis Highway, and then the plane touched down with a bump and the engines howled in reverse. As they rolled down the runway Hudson caught a glimpse of a huge sign by the highway adorned with Elvis' mug, a shot from his early Las Vegas days. The sign proclaimed simply: "Viva Reunification."

Elvis was now 64, lived permanently in California, where he mostly read about history, philosophy, and astrology, and he had finally allowed those famous sideburns to gray. The C.S.A. had forgiven him for leaving the country years ago for Hollywood, and he was in fact the only American who could claim citizenship in both nations. That was the power of turning crappy songs and movies into an art form. Having reached the magical age plateau created by Paul McCartney, and ahead of McCartney, the ex-Beatle re-issued "When I'm 64" and dedicated it to Elvis. George Harrison and Ringo Starr also played on the new cut, and Yoko Ono offered to fly to England to advise the Fab Three on how to improve the song. Paul diplomatically declined and suggested that perhaps Yoko's unusual and unique talents, which would be wasted on mere music, coupled with her experience with things breaking up, might best be best directed toward helping the two Americas reunify. Yoko, delighted by the suggestion, said she'd get right on it. Grail once dreamt that Yoko was having sex with Regis Philbin, who quizzed her at the end with, "Is that your final orgasm?"

The Elvis aura, which thankfully never included Yoko Ono, had never diminished in the C.S.A. Born in Mississippi and raised in Memphis, and a C.S.A. army veteran to boot, Elvis possessed an ironclad pedigree and the C.S.A. Congress was almost giddy the day in 1975 when it restored his citizenship and he lurched through "Love Me Tender" on the floor of Congress to thank them. There were a lot of misty eyes in that audience, although commentators wondered if the tears were produced by the song or the sight of Elvis' massive belt buckle holding back his great marbled stomach like a tiny Hoover Dam.

"Amazing," Hudson said. "With Elvis in the fold I guess reunification can't fail."

Leslie looked out the window. "Did you see one of the new signs? I wondered when they'd get them up. Elvis has agreed to sing at the reunification celebration."

Grail smirked.

"Don't laugh," she said. "Elvis is still huge, even at 64."

"His belly is pretty huge alright."

"Yeah, but you know what? When I was in New York I heard Henry Kissinger refer to Elvis as maybe the single most unifying icon of our time. Henry Kissinger, for God's sake."

"What does that mean?"

"Unifying icon?" she said. "I have no idea. But if Kissinger said it it must be true."

The plane reached the gate and ostensibly intelligent, reasonable people, Hudson noted, became maniacal idiots tussling with overhead baggage as they jockeyed for position in the aisle as though it was lunch time at a reform school for the potentially criminal. How very curious that people so sensitive about their personal spaces when they get on a plane are so willing to mash against each other like sardines when it's time to get off. Grail and Leslie waited until the crunch was over before leisurely strolling toward the terminal.

"What about that drink, Leslie? Do you have time?"

"Sorry, but I don't. Not now, anyway. They want me at state right away, and Finch doesn't like his people to have alcohol on their breaths until *after* work."

"Shoot. I guess I'm stuck with this Mallory Wade character, and you miss the chance to rehabilitate a known Lee hater."

"Oh, you don't get off the hook that easily, Grail. There's a reception sponsored by State tomorrow. I'm sure Wade will take you, and I'll be there to make sure you don't sing The Battle Hymn of the Republic, or something equally as barbarous."

"I can't sing. Not a note. That's Fat Elvis' job."

"That's right, and he's been invited. Here's your chance to get his autograph."

"Or slip some Slim Fast in his drink."

"You *are* determined to get in trouble in my country, aren't you Dr. Hudson?"

"I'm just a harmless professor, Leslie. But I 'm determined to see some of this country."

"That's Wade's job. I'll introduce you two, but then I have to run.

They stood near the Dixie Airways counter by the gate, but Leslie didn't see Wade anywhere.

"Will he be some dweeby guy with a sign that says "Grail Hudson?"

"Doubt it," she said. "He's probably studied your picture until he can see you in his sleep. He really should be here by now."

"Maybe he's still studying my picture and forgot. Will Kissinger be at the reception?"

"Of course. He's part of the U.S. contingent. He's been advising Clinton, you know."

"I know. Our state boys and girls briefed me in New York. I want to see Kissinger and Elvis kicking back together. Icon to icon, of course. Belly to belly."

Leslie checked her watch nervously and then scanned the crowd, but no Wade. Finally she knew she had to go if she was to make her meeting.

"Grail, I'm out of time. Gotta go. I'm sure Wade will be here any second. Traffic can be heavy right now, especially with all this rain."

"What's he look like?"

"Like you envisioned—silk underwear and a pudgy pinkie in the air. Usually a bow tie. I'm so sorry to leave you like this, but—"

"No problem. I'll see you at that reception."

"Absolutely," Leslie called over her shoulder, and then she disappeared into a collage of color and people as "Dixie" came over the terminal loudspeakers.

Chapter 12

▼

Elvis was in a funk. A fluid purple don't-step-on-my-blue-suede-shoes, return-to-sender, suspicious-minds sort of funk.

It just hadn't been fun yet, man, since arriving the day before in pouring rain. Elvis didn't go out in the rain because of the impurities—not to mention radioactivity from all those nuclear tests, man—and it hadn't really stopped raining since he stepped off Gladys, his private jet. He had read about acid rain, man, and wasn't taking any chances.

He leaned back in his chair, pushed close to the window of the Confederate Plaza Radisson presidential suite and fingered a chunky diamond ring on a finger. Twenty-first floor, man. Best view of the city, baby. But no action. Just sitting here waiting for the rain to stop. Man, the colonel would know what to do about this. He'd set something up, man, that would be fun. Maybe do a movie, or make a quick trip to Vegas.

No. No, Colonel Parker was long dead of a heart attack. Elvis knew that. Well, sometimes he did and sometimes he didn't. Some days he did and some days he didn't. This was one of those days when he did and he didn't.

Rain streaked down the window and Elvis watched drops race each other to the bottom. Man, where was Red? Where was Sonny? Joe Esposito? The Guys. Long gone and finally living their own lives away from Elvis, who got religion, of sorts, after cheating death back in 77 at Graceland, now long abandoned and a museum to his life, when God Hisownself—or someone remarkably like him—strolled into the Memphis hospital and leaned over Elvis, bloated and marble white on the gurney, and said, "Elvis, you have been fucking up big time, son, and now it's time to choose whether you die this instant or get a life that's worth a damn and not some pharmaceutical odyssey."

To everyone's surprise, he straightened up. With the help of Betty Sue Thomas, a pretty nurse who had cared for him at the hospital and who was pragmatic enough to know an opportunity when she saw it, Elvis got straight. Betty Sue stayed up with him when he saw snakes crawling walls, when he sweated through his pajamas and whimpered like an infant and pissed his pants. She held him and brought him truckloads of books on the Shroud of Turin and Native American religion and all schools of philosophy and astrology. She grabbed him by the lapels of his pajamas and virtually screamed into his face that his saintly parents, the beloved Gladys and the devoted Vernon, would not forgive him in heaven should he fail to win this battle, and slowly he began to accept it as true.

Betty Sue somehow got his backbone back in him and he fired the Memphis Mafia—generously, of course: new cars, cash, some rings. Betty Sue became his confidant, mother figure, nurse, and even his lover when he could. No more massive doses of Demerol, no more uppers to perform, no more downers to sleep. It had been a rough, ugly transition from a pill-popping egomaniac to something resembling a human being that could actually go out in the sunlight, drive a car, even balance a checkbook. Not that he needed to balance a checkbook. Not ever. But Betty Sue showed him how just the same.

Of course, shocking Elvis back from zombie land was not without its damage. He could not be left on his own for great periods of time and so Betty Sue hired an ex-marine turned social worker named Clark Ritchie to be his personal assistant. Clark hovered in the background, ready to provide direction if Elvis drifted, to be a sort of man Friday. Clark had the room next to Elvis's suite and was trying to give Elvis as much space as he could on orders from Betty Sue, who decided not to come along because she wanted Elvis to feel he was on one of those great adventures he would abruptly launch back in the old days that seemed to energize his wandering mind and give it focus. Clark was there to make sure the famous Elvis focus didn't get too adventurous or self-destructive.

At 64 Elvis still colored his hair but had allowed the sideburns to sprout some salt and pepper. A concession to age that was hard for him at first. He was pot-bellied and still insisted on elaborate costumes sometimes, such as capes and Edwardian jackets; but the stomach didn't matter to his fans. He was Elvis, he was E, he was still the torrid singer that prompted announcers to say "Elvis has left the building," and he still had the quick, infectious grin and mischievous eyes that seemed always to make women swoon.

Elvis grabbed the remote control, fired up the TV, and found one of his old ones—"Follow That Dream." In the movie Young Elvis hefted a Thompson submachine gun. Old Elvis smiled and remembered the feel of the gun in his hands. What was that Beatles song? "Happiness is a Warm Gun." Yeah, man.

Later, when Clark came in with his clothes for the C.S.A. reception that evening, Elvis just nodded absentmindedly at the choice of jacket Clark offered—one of the many Edwardian jackets—and sighed, remembering Young Elvis and the Thompson. Back in the old days he'd have had a pair of Colt .45s tucked in his waistband.

Back in the old days he might just have shot the TV out.

Yeah, baby.

Chapter 13

▼

Wade masturbated in the sleek, Confederate gray limo on the way to the airport, not quite sure whether the driver could hear or see him. There was a window between them and the shade had been drawn, but he had put his trench coat on his lap just in case. Halfway across the Pickett Bridge Wade had his relief and eased back into the plush upholstery. He had just come from the Radisson, where he checked on Elvis. When exactly had he become the C.S.A.'s babysitter for VIPs?

Elvis had been moody, difficult, and at one point drew Wade aside and asked him for a gun. A gun for Christ's sake! A .45 would do nicely, but he would settle for a 9mm, explaining that it was just to stick in the waistband of his trousers, for protection, that he was an expert with firearms as well as karate. He even demonstrated his favorite karate stances to Wade, who had a very trying time explaining that the C.S.A., unlike the violent U.S., had finally won the battle against the insane N.R.A., which had been broken up, its leaders deported. Charlton Heston had been informed he was not welcome to visit. Public pressure had helped create real gun control laws. The murder rate had plummeted. Not even Elvis could carry a gun, especially at a reception that the president would attend. Wade pointed out that when Elvis had showed up at the New White House in New York to visit Nixon in 73 the Secret Service had disarmed him.

"I was at Nixon's funeral," Elvis said. "Wore the badge he got me. C'mon, man, the gun will balance my walk. A man's walk is pretty important. Did you catch my walk in G.I. Blues with Juliet Prowse?"

"Sorry, Mr. Presley. Somehow I missed that."

"Call me E, man, everybody does. Well, they used to anyway."

"Sure, E. How did you walk in G.I. Blues?"

"Like this, baby," and Elvis tried to strut across the room, but his bad back made him look like a chicken with lumbago.

"Did that tickle Miss Prowse?"

"Man, did it ever. Mercy!"

"I see." Wade glanced at Clark, who had the detached but still aware look of someone who has seen a train wreck more than once. Clark produced what appeared to be a .45, but to Wade's relief, he whispered that it was a replica.

"His pacifier," Clark said quietly.

Elvis stuck the gun in the waistband of his pants and the old famous grin with unlimited charm stitched across his face like it had a zipper, and then he was back in front of the TV. Clark walked Wade to the door.

"Don't worry, Mr. Wade, I'll disarm him before the reception."

Over his shoulder Wade heard Elvis yell, "Clark, get Red and Sonny up here. I need to practice my new karate moves so I can show them to President Carter tonight."

"Red and Sonny are in California, E. Remember? They wrote a book about you. You didn't like it. Remember?"

"Yeah. OK. Well, how about Chuck Norris? Will he be there?"

Clark looked at Wade.

"Actually, I think he will."

Clark held the door open. He shook hands with Clark and saw Elvis retrieve the replica .45, point it at the TV, and yell, "Pow!"

And then he finally looked at his watch and knew he had missed Hudson. Damn! How could he screw up like that? The limo had crossed over the Pickett Bridge to the Virginia side, but Hudson's plane had been down for 30 minutes. The rain garnished his frustration with sheets thumping loudly on the limo. It sounded like pebbles thrown on a tin roof. Cascades of water swooshed away from the limo's flanks as it slithered through pools soaking Jeff Davis Highway. He glimpsed one of the Elvis signs, E's face smiling innocently through the rain. How many people really knew that Elvis was about a quarter past bughouse?

There was a TGI Friday's near the gate, and that's where Wade found Grail, who was drinking a Bell's Amber Ale and reading the *Washington Post*. There were two suitcases at Grail's feet. Wade realized that Hudson had had time to find baggage claim, wait for the bags to shoot onto the carousel, and then heft them up the escalator to the restaurant. This was all so unpardonable, and Wade wasn't sure how he could make it up to the man.

"Doctor Hudson, I presume."

Grail looked up from his paper and didn't say anything at first. He studied Wade, who was wearing a yellow polka dot bow tie. Wade's collar looked too tight and beads of sweat glistened on his shiny forehead. Grail wanted to appear annoyed but could not after the pint of beer.

"Yes, I'm Grail Hudson."

"Mallory Wade, at your service, doctor. I am so sorry about this confusion—"

"It's OK." Grail tried a faint smile. "Please, call me Grail. That doctor business always makes me feel old. Like I should be able to do bypass surgery, or at least CPR."

"Excellent," Wade said. "Grail it is. I see you have your bags. Great. The delay is unpardonable, I know. Please accept my apology again—I was tied up with someone difficult, and traffic was heavy."

"And the rain," Grail said. "Does it ever stop?"

Wade leaned closer. "You know, there are people who say it means the end of the world, and that we'll soon be needing an ark."

"Really?" Grail said, trying to appear disinterested.

"Or that God is angry about something down here," Wade added. It was intended to be an icebreaker, humorous perhaps, but Wade was surprised to hear it sound more like a challenge to go to a political level of dialogue.

Grail leaned over and picked up his bags. "Do you suppose people say that during the rainy season in Seattle, or Portland?"

"There's no reunification going on in Seattle or Portland," Wade said, a little embarrassed by his sharp tone. He did not know where it was coming from. He wondered if he had submerged antagonistic feelings toward Hudson, who after all was famous for criticizing Wade's homeland.

"True enough," Grail said, bags in hand. "Shall we go?"

"Yes, of course," Mallory said. "Here, let me have one of those."

On the escalator Mallory found himself unable to abandon whatever it was his subconscious was serving up to him. "What I meant about the rain was that some people actually see it as a comment on reunification. Not me, of course."

"Right." Grail stared at Wade without expression for a very long moment, and then they were off the escalator and outside. The limo was at the curb. Wade's driver took Grail's luggage. The rain showed no sign of slackening.

"It's amazing, isn't it?" Mallory said. "It's been this way for weeks. A break here and there, and then down it comes again."

"Has the Potomac broke its banks?" Grail asked.

"Several times. Flooding all the way up to the Vietnam Memorial. Can't blame some folks for thinking we'll all just float away."

Inside the limo Grail said, "I'm curious, Mallory. Which side do you see the rain paranoia aimed at?"

"Which side?"

"Yeah. Is God pissed at you for wanting to reunify? Or has God rained on your parade to discourage the anti-reunification folks? See what I mean?"

Wade did not see, not exactly, but nodded as though he did. The limo lurched away from the curb through pools of water onto the slick highway. The silence between them was awkward, almost like being summoned before the great Finch, Wade thought. As they crossed the Pickett Bridge Grail broke the silence: "George Pickett. A fascinating romantic. But a broken man after Gettysburg. Absolutely shattered. He always blamed Lee, you know."

Mallory decided not to tangle with Grail over Lee, perhaps as partial payment for being late. And he was still obsessed about their earlier conversation on the rain. As the limo pulled up at Grail's hotel, Mallory said, "OK, so you were saying the rain doesn't have to be negative? That it's not a sign against reunification?"

"Exactly." Grail got out and the driver offered to carry the bags inside, but Grail thanked him and took them himself. He started into the lobby but turned back to Mallory.

"Maybe the rain is cleansing the C.S.A.," Grail said. "You know, getting it ready for future greatness. As a member of the union again, of course—not as a separate nation."

"Yes, of course," Mallory called, but not sounding convinced.

Grail took a step, then turned once more. "And then again, maybe it's something else altogether."

"What?" Wade said eagerly.

"Maybe it's just a hell of a lot of rain."

Chapter 14

▼

Ventura Pier on a clear, sunny morning, the wind still someplace up the coast, perhaps scouring the beaches at Pismo or Morrow Bay, and the Channel Islands were visible for a change. The noisy breakfast crowd, a battalion of Hawaiian shirts and sun dresses and sunglasses, had evaporated at Eric Ericcson's, and the tanned, blonde legion of buff boys and girls in tight blacks shorts and white shirts and blouses rattled plates and glasses as they prepared for lunch. Bold seagulls rummaged through the remains on the tables outside facing the beach, and a chatty one snatched a fat packet of butter and ate it, wrapper and all, while perched on the pier railing as a Japanese tourist took its picture.

Wad Upshot left Ericcson's and glided handsomely toward the end of the pier on long legs that had won many a 220 and long jump 20 years ago for Robert E. Lee High School in Arlington, Virginia. Seagulls trailed him discretely, hoping for a handout. The pier was deserted except for two old fishermen with a bottle between them. The Pacific was blue and calm. Surfer's Point to the right was caressed by limp waves as a gaggle of surfers stared in disappointment. On the beach below clumps of buttery bodies sprawled in various stages of real as well as pretend relaxation.

He reached the end of the pier and placed his back against the railing. Ventura was spread out before him: pricey houses infesting brown hills. The Sierra Madre Mountains lurked somewhere beyond the city, if it could be called that. A constant parade of human pretension sauntered up and down the beach promenade, occasionally changing course and cruising up California Street in search of a café or bar from which to do mostly nothing at all.

Wad—he'd accepted the name and didn't try to insist on Robert anymore—had lived for two years in Ventura after ten down in the sordid sprawl of L.A. Twelve years in Southern California was a long time, long enough to forget that it was, after all, a pissant rogue nation unto itself obsessed with image. Twelve years was enough time for almost anyone to become just another neon fish swimming along in the cocaine current. Yet after twelve years—ten as the infamous porn star—Wad somehow never ceased to be amazed by how hard many Southern Californians worked to appear relaxed. They literally worked up a sweat to project cool.

He had moved north to Ventura after the porn business because he didn't want to run into anyone from L.A. Ten years of first acting, then directing, and finally producing fuck films had netted him some money and he had bought land outside Ventura. Progress had grown cancer-like to his property and now the land was worth even more. That was old Virginia in him: get some land. He had come to realize that old Virginia still had a flame inside him, and twelve years among sillyass narcissists had not been enough to change that. Porn icon Ron Jeremy had told him he was crazy. Why leave the good life in LA? All appetites are served there, Jeremy said, and his appetites for food and sex never suffered.

Jeremy had even hinted that Wad couldn't leave LA, that once in the porn family one could never leave it; but Wad had finally heard enough and told Jeremy that's what Charlie Manson once said, and hey, maybe you could drop a few pounds, Ron, so people don't keep calling you a hedgehog. Ten years of bad judgment were forever preserved on video and Wad knew it would follow him to his grave, but he had accepted the albatross and was prepared to live with it. Unlike Jeremy—and especially the silly, smutty Howard Stern, who once interviewed Wad—he'd outgrown the small boy fascination with sex.

He was no longer in an arrested state of adolescence like Jeremy and Stern, and could move on, even if it meant trailing a decade all too well documented.

Wad didn't know exactly when it was he had grown up. He just knew that at some point he looked around at the women so strangely willing to be degraded and deprived of their own pleasure to satisfy a dark male need to dominate and inflict humiliation, and the young men, mostly, who so easily could not see the women as anything other than orifices to be used in any way, and realized how strange it was that he had not seen it sooner. Except that in the beginning he was still in his twenties, adventurous, uninhibited, horny, had the looks and equipment for the job, and just sort of fell into it. Fucking. It was an excellent concept. Even now. There was a difference, though, between him and the porn lifers, and he had felt it stronger each day after he left the business: Southern California, indeed the whole U.S. with advertising gone mad, unregulated, and allowed to be a sort of unofficial social engineering arm of the government, perpetuated women as objects to be molded into whatever role suited men.

It had stung horribly when the C.S.A. had stripped him of his citizenship shortly after his porn career began. Two years ago, when he left porn for good, he had applied to visit his country. He was denied. Now he was going back for the first time in twelve years, but his visa had been granted only because his brother Jeff had cancer. He couldn't believe the news. His brother was gravely ill and there was nothing he could do. He wasn't sure how his Mom would be. They had written a few letters, exchanged a few phone calls. Some e-mail. It was awkward. Well, thinking about it didn't do any good. He had to get down to L.A. and catch his plane and then take it all from there. He would be in Washington that evening. With luck it would be the first step to a different, better life. He could sell his California land and would be well off. He was prepared to stay in Virginia. He wanted it back. The C.S.A. sometimes forgave its wayward sons and he was hoping for mercy. But the first thing was to become Robert Whitfield again. No more Wad.

Robert went home and packed, and then he drove south on 101. He stopped for gas in Camarillo and then for coffee in Woodland Hills. The kid behind the counter at Starbucks recognized him and gave him a thumbs up.

"Awesome, dude," the kid said. "Wad Upshot rules. Man, all those babes."

Porn had become just another social institution manufacturing money in Southern California and Robert had helped make it so. For some kids in La La Land going off to porn was like going off to UCLA or USC. He winced at the thought, but managed a smile for the kid, who asked him how he could break into porn. The kid was maybe 17 and had a gold ring in his nose. Probably came from an affluent family with a big house, tennis court, pool, jacuzzi, and matching BMWs for his parents, who were either software designers or owned some business that guaranteed television and the local upscale mall had raised their children. Southern Californian kids seemed to regard porn as not much different than a part-time job with great perks. Something to do while waiting for something to happen. Sex was just another layer of fashion to them, like baseball caps worn backwards and thong bikinis.

"Wad Upshot is such a cool name, dude," the kid said, eager to please. "Like, hey, what name could I use? Myself, I'd be a bitching porn dude, dude.

"Truly?"

"Absolutely," the kid said. "Got the equipment, ace."

"That's so commendable," Robert said. He sipped the coffee. "How about Biff Upchuck?"

The boy pondered the name and looked confused, not quite sure what Upchuck meant, but was finally happy it had "up" in it.

"Hey, that's a good one, dude," he said. "Biff Upchuck. Awesome, man."

"It suits you," Robert said. "It really does."

"Really? For sure?"

"For sure," Robert said. "When I look at you, upchuck is definitely the first thing I think about."

"Yeah? Wow, man, the great Wad Upshot has given me my porn name." He leaned over the counter closer to Robert. "You know, this Starbucks shit is just a temporary gig anyhow. I'm, like, destined for stardom, dude."

"Everybody in Southern California is," Robert said.

"Yeah, man. Hey, like, that's so true."

As Robert started to leave the kid said, "So, Wad, do you have any porn tips for me?"

"Tips?"

"Yeah. You know, techniques. Hey, not that I'm a slacker in that department. Just ask Heather." He smacked the butt of a pretty blonde, tan teenager as she went by with a load of bagels.

"You're gross," she said. "And we're out of decaf."

"Got it under control," the kid said.

"Get your brain damage under control," she said, making a face.

The kid gave her another smack and turned back to the counter, but Robert was already out the door, and he wasn't looking back.

Somewhere over Kansas or Missouri at about 30,000 feet, while sipping California chardonnay and skimming *The New Yorker*, Robert had the opening moments of his epiphany. It came from a cloud shaped like a cat's paw. He had watched the cloud a long time and wondered why he thought it was a cat's paw, or why people saw clouds as anything besides clouds. But this was definitely a cat's paw, and it kept opening and closing gently. It was only wind currents, of course, or the jetstream, or whatever else lurks at 30,000 feet, but still, Robert saw a cat's paw gently clenching and releasing. He accepted a second chardonnay and gazed as the cloud began to fall into another shape, this time a face. But whose face? God's? He wasn't sure, and he found himself missing the cat's paw. That was the exact moment epiphany struck.

There are signs everywhere if people will only look, and Robert believed that. The problem is that most people never look, or are too consumed with consuming, for example, to notice what's going around them, on simpler planes, that are more valuable than anything material. He saw the contractions of the cat's paw as even a sign from God. Was there a God? Would God forgive him his sins? If so, Robert was a lot closer to it, he, she at 30,000 feet than he was porking babes for the camera at Venice Beach. Ironically, he could have seen a cat's paw contracting from ground level, but there, he was too consumed, like everyone else in the United States of Getting Ahead. It would have been there, a slient beacon in the sky, but he wouldn't have noticed.

Robert's palms began to sweat as he realized what it all meant: he must redeem himself, reinvent himself, save himself. And that salvation—and it was very much alvation he wanted—was possible by helping others. The cat's paw was calling him. It was a message. A warning, too: doors open and close. Opportunites are offered and retracted. Open, close. Open, close. Come in or stay out. Go in, stay out. Seize the moment or let it pass.

But do what? He looked again out the window and saw land, dry and brown, far below, and there were no more clouds at all. He glanced across the aisle out that window, and others, but there were no clouds. No cat paws. No more messages? Of course not. He was on his own now. Time to bring the most crucial part to the equation offered. A direction, a plan, a thesis, a goal. His thoughts had become fuzzy and he knew he would sleep a while, but the direction was clear: he would sell his land for a good price and find something worthwhile to sink it in back in Virginia. He would become a Virginian again. He could establish a foundation. He could produce historical films for the C.S.A. My God, he could become legit, a director and producer in his homeland, and he would take care of his brother. And his mother. And ask for forgiveness from The South.

In his dream Robert saw James Longstreet and George Pickett making a porn movie, circa 1863. Women in curls and hoop skirts. The generals wearing spurs that clanked and great shiny boots to their knees and nothing else except their hats. Swords discarded, but great erections sword-like. There were no cameras then, of course, but that didn't stop the two Confederate generals from banging everything in sight. It didn't stop Robert from being their director. Where was Robert E. Lee? Ah, well, a man with the dignity of Lee would never stoop so low. There was a message in that.

Robert had just reached the scene where Longstreet and Pickett, still nude except for hats, boots, and spurs, clanked toward Lee's tent to persuade the grand old gentleman to forget the debacle at Gettysburg and join them in their antics, when he was pulled from the dream by someone squeezing his shoulder.

"Cut," Robert said instinctively, his eyes still half-shut and not focusing. The hand squeezed again and Robert's eyes fluttered. He tried to focus on the bearded face, which was clear and then blurry again.

"General Lee?" Robert said, still crossing the bridge to reality.

"General Lee?" the bearded voice repeated.

Robert was awake, and the bearded face was grinning. Robert looked at the face and then out his window: no clouds.

"I'm John Gordon," the man said. "You were moaning in your sleep."

"Really?" Robert said. There had been a Confederate general named John Gordon, but he wasn't in Robert's dream. He studied the man and realized he had been sitting across the aisle since they boarded in L.A. "Did I say anything?"

"Nothing much. Sounds mostly."

"Thanks for waking me. I was having a strange dream."

"Listen," John Gordon said, his voice low, conspiratorial. He glanced around quickly and leaned closer to Robert. "I didn't want to cause a scene or anything, but I recognized you." The man leaned back, looking very satisfied.

"I see," Robert said, figuring it was another porn wannabee. Has everyone on the planet seen a porn movie? It occurred to Robert that there were people who didn't know the capital of South Dakota but did know what his dick looked like.

"You're Wad Upshot." John Gordon said the name in almost a whisper, and then glanced quickly around to see if anyone was watching.

"I *was* Wad Upshot. I buried him several years ago in a bar north of Malibu. I'm Robert Whitfield. Always have been, actually."

"Yeah, I know you're retired, Wad."

"It's Robert." He leaned close to John. "John, retired usually implies the completion of a happy career. I didn't retire. I walked away."

"That's why I'm glad I ran into you," he said. "I write for *People* magazine, Wad—I mean, Robert. Sorry about that. Look, I'd like to talk to you about why you left the porn industry."

"Why? Aren't your readers more interested in Oprah Winfrey's latest diet?"

"Oprah's big,—no doubt about it. I mean as a celebrity, of course. Say, didn't you once appear on her show? Yeah, I remember that. You and Nina Hartley. Man, that gal has some butt. But I guess I don't have to tell *you* that."

"The little narcissist," Robert said quietly. "Yeah, that was us alright. We were liberating the masses."

"Cool. So, do you see much of her these days? If you know what I mean," he said, smirking.

"Oprah?"

"No, Nina Hartley."

"Sorry, it's been years.

"Really?

"A lifetime ago, Johnny Boy. Why not leave it at that?"

"It's news, Robert. People want to know."

"Is this an interview, John?"

"Well, any time you're talking to me, you're talking to the magazine. But for the people. Always for the people."

"You're just a public servant? Like Oprah?"

"I'm just a humble journalist. Well, maybe not so humble."

"Ma'am," Robert called to the attendant as she passed by. "Could I have some more wine?"

"Me, too," John said, digging in a pocket. "My treat."

"Then it is an interview," Robert said, and thought, why not? A little publicity from a major magazine might just be the way to show people he was a changed man. It might even help his case for regaining C.S.A. citizenship. He wanted that badly. He didn't want California anymore, or the exile it mandated. Spin control. If people say they're something and it appears in a magazine or on TV, soon everyone accepts them as that. It worked for Madonna, who claimed she was an actress and a singer, and after a while people started buying it. It worked fabulously for Regis Philbin and Kathie Lee Something. And the Republican Party. People even believed that Shaquille O'Neal was a basketball player. Hadn't he said he was countless times? The beauty of it was that Robert wouldn't have to lie. Here was his chance to proclaim himself a Virginian once again, to be a Virginian right down to the tip of his—shoe.

They sipped their wine. Robert felt a renewed sense of purpose. "What's in Washington, John? Got a hot story there?"

"Reunification," he said. "That's the hottest story going."

"You'll be rubbing elbows with *Time* and *Newsweek*."

"And Elvis."

"Elvis?"

"That's who I'm really going to see. We've arranged for the first interview The King has given in ten years. He's eager to spruce up his image."

Elvis. Robert sensed the potential. Elvis was somehow able to transcend everything. His mere presence in Washington was good luck for reunification talks.

From what he knew, Elvis was actually sort of prematurely senile, or maybe crazy, and yet it was possible to orbit The King like a compliant satellite and absorb the warm sunshine rays of goodwill that followed the Buddha of rock and roll everywhere.

"Well, Johnny old pal—how about two birds for the price of one? How about we sit down in Washington and do a formal interview with pictures?"

"Really? The whole nine yards?"

"Sure. Absolutely. You've got a photographer around somewhere, don't you?"

"She's already there, shooting the city for background." John rubbed his chin and squinted. "I thought you weren't interested in being interviewed."

"Did I say I wasn't interested? I was still groggy from that dream. But there's a condition."

"What condition?"

"Can you get me in to see Elvis?"

"Probably. Why do you want to see Elvis?"

Robert tossed down the rest of his wine. "Oh, let's just say I'm a big fan. Is it a deal?"

John hesitated for a moment, then offered his hand. "Yeah, it's a deal."

The plane began its descent. Robert looked out and saw the Potomac, swollen and silver. The pilot came over the intercom and announced there was a break in the rain. Robert smiled and hummed a few bars of "Dixie."

Chapter 15

▼

Grail had hung up his clothes and retreated to a sumptuous leather chair in the Raddison lobby, away from the intrusions of telephones and C.S.A. State Department toadies, and even the incessant rain, which though it came down in sheets outside could barely be heard in the snug ambience of the quiet and majestic lobby. He had been thinking again of his father—no smoky six-foot Ts floating like a jellyfish this time, just the hard reality that the man did actually exist, was alive, lived somewhere, had a life, and Grail knew almost nothing about him. Grail distracted himself as best he could with the *Washington Post,* though he strongly suspected it would take something more physical than reading. Still, Grail had begun to relax, to not *think*.

After a while, and quite randomly, he looked up from the *Post* and blinked in disbelief. No, he thought, it could not be. But indeed he could have sworn, just for a puzzling moment, that Elvis Presley darted out of one of the elevators. Though cloaked in a full length dark raincoat, a Chicago Bears cap jammed tight on his head, the man suggested the unmistakable Elvis profile of sideburns, big glasses, and big hair—now gray, but still a great mane. Elvis, or whoever it was, looked both ways and then scurried off.

Elvis Schmelvish. Grail frowned and fidgeted in his chair. Did he need a drink? He did cast a questioning glance across the lobby at the entrance of the Gettysburg Lounge. Or perhaps he was just tired, his brain undisciplined as a result and susceptible to confusion. Had it really been Elvis? After all, he was in town to sing at the Reunification Ball. Grail yawned. No way. Surely the man would have his own secret entrance. Security teams to whisk him in and out of limos behind the hotel. A secret elevator? Grail dismissed that as too James Bondish, even for Elvis Aaron Presley, the King of rock and roll, who Grail was sure would not be walking around in public. Grail picked up the paper again; but almost immediately something in him wouldn't let go of it, couldn't let go. Damnit! He jumped up and just had to know, just as some people had to know if they had left the iron on, or the front door unlocked, the back gate open, the water running.

Grail leaned over a low wall of Swedish ivy behind his chair and saw a carpeted hallway leading past the hotel hair salon. Whoever the man was, Elvis or not, he was slowly making his way toward a hotel exit far down the hallway, occasionally looking over his shoulder but seemingly unconcerned and in no hurry. His gait was relaxed and casual, a saunter as though without a care in the world. At the door the man stopped and leaned into it, but did not open it right away. It was as if he was taking in the outside world skeptically, suddenly unsure of whether to actually go out or not.

Grail had positioned himself at the corner to the hallway and slyly looked around, just as the man pushed fully against the door handle and stepped outside. "What the hell am I doing?" Grail said loud enough that a young woman passing by shot him a frown. Grail hurried down the hallway to the door and peeked carefully outside. The man had not yet reached the street corner. The rain had stopped, awfully mysteriously and abruptly, Grail noted, and when the man looked back once Grail nonetheless knew it really was Elvis. The king of rock and roll was actually wearing a Chicago Bears cap and a trench coat, and was sneaking toward Pennsylvania Avenue.

Fascinated and happy to be doing something to take his thoughts off his father, Grail followed Elvis for several blocks. It was as if Grail was drawn by a magnet, powerless to resist. Occasionally someone would seem to recognize Elvis, but the King was in gear now, strolling with confidence, the Bears cap pulled down a little tighter, but clearly enjoying his foray into reality. The sun had even peeked from around a cloud, compelling people to look up as if discovering it for the first time. Grail tailed Elvis for a few more blocks with absolutely no clue why he was doing it. Finally a woman did stop Elvis for the inevitable autograph, and while he signed Elvis cast an inquisitive glance toward Grail, who pretended to window shop in front of an Eddie Bauer store. Before a knot of fans could form Elvis abruptly crossed the street and slipped into a stream of pedestrians unaware of the king in their midst, but an alert Grail noticed as Elvis ducked into Starbucks.

It began to rain again as Grail crossed the street and entered Starbucks. He stood just inside the door and tried to conceal himself behind a shelf of coffee beans as he scanned the room for Elvis. The king was nowhere to be seen. As he edged past the entrance to the bathrooms he felt something hard pressed into his back and felt a hand on his shoulder, and then he was gently but firmly pulled back into the shelter of the bathroom alcove. The hand released him and Grail whirled around and faced Elvis, who had a pistol barely protruding from inside his trench coat.

"Good Lord," Grail said, then wondering if it was the appropriate response for being held up at gunpoint by Elvis Presley.

Elvis flashed the famous sneer, his lip trembling like it had in so many beach movies and drug-enhanced Vegas performances, but he slowly put the gun down and then tucked it into the waist band of his pants.

"Don't fret, man," Elvis said. "It's just a replica .45. It don't shoot. Clark thinks I don't know the difference, but I do." The sneer again, but friendly. He seemed to sense Grail was not a threat.

"Who's Clark?" Grail said, puzzled, still a little awed to be lurking in a bathroom alcove at Starbucks with Elvis Presley.

"Clark's one of my guys. Hell, he's my only guy. Why are you following me, man? Are you with the CIA, or do you just want an autograph?"

"The CIA? Lord no. Did you really think—"

"Didn't know what to think. I have to be careful."

"Is the CIA really following you?"

"Maybe," Elvis said, glancing down at his shoes. "The U.S.A. has always held it against me some that I took C.S.A. citizenship. But hell, man—I'm a southern boy."

Grail was speechless. His mouth opened once but he didn't know what to say. He began to smile, to acknowledge that although he had never given Elvis much thought in his entire life, now he was sensing what the king's legions of fans always knew: the man was simply one of the most charismatic persons ever to stride the earth, even now, at 64, paunchy and faded, the sideburns mostly white, the rest of the hair long since gone gray.

"So, man, want to get some coffee?" Elvis said. "Starbucks has the best. Sometimes I sneak out in disguise back in L.A. and have a cup at a Starbucks in Beverly Hills."

"Don't people recognize you at all?"

"Naw, man. In L.A. I wear a fake beard and stuff. Besides, in Beverly Hills there's so many famous people a guy in a cap and beard is just another dude in the background."

They bought coffee and Elvis guided Grail to a table in the back of the room, partially hidden by ferns. Several people regarded Elvis suspiciously, but no one seemed to recognize him.

Elvis sipped his coffee. "Yeah, man—I love Starbucks. So, man, like I was saying—who are you?"

"Grail Hudson." They shook hands.

"Are you a fan?" Elvis looked hopeful.

"No." Grail immediately regretted it. "I didn't mean to suggest I wasn't, that I—what I mean is I know who you are. I've seen some of your movies and all that, it's just—"

"S'okay, man." Elvis was grinning. "Not everybody's a fan. So, what do you do, Grail?"

"I'm a professor."

"No fooling?" Elvis seemed genuinely impressed.

"Yes, that's right. I'm a history professor at the University of Illinois. And I apologize for following you. I don't know why I was. I saw you come out of the elevator at the Raddison—I was sitting in the lobby—and I guess I didn't believe it was you. I guess I just wanted to find out. I don't know."

"Hah! You're a fan after all." Elvis said, and then he suddenly appeared pensive, seemed to be searching for something, and then it came to him: "Grail Hudson? I know that name, man. Sure I do." He leaned forward. "You wrote *Birth of a Rebel Nation*. Yeah, baby. I read a lot of books, but I remember that one. It's brilliant, man, But you were a little hard on old Bobby Lee, as I recall."

"Yes, I hear that a lot." Grail was truly impressed: his book had been read by Elvis Presley, and he thinks it's *brilliant*. But then Grail wondered if that was actually a good thing, being judged brilliant by a garish old icon like Elvis. Still, it was great to just hear someone had read it other than nervous C.S.A politicians.

"You know," Elvis continued, "I recall a particular line from the book. Let's see, it went something like, uh, but the Confederacy, now a legitimate nation after a war that seemed to promise it would never be a nation, must now not fail to win the other war, the one for a legitimate national identity. Did I get that right?"

"Yes," Grail said. "That sounds word for word, I believe. I'm flattered."

"Well hell's bells, Grail. I reckon I'm the one who ought to be asking for an autograph." Elvis was beaming, and Grail beamed back, but after an awkward moment Grail realized Elvis was waiting for something, and it dawned on Grail after a few more seconds of staring at Elvis' incredibly white teeth that it really was an autograph Elvis was waiting for. He had even fished a pen out of his trench coat.

"I have a copy of my book back at the hotel," Grail said. "Would you like me to sign it for you? Would you accept a copy as a gift?"

"Man, would I ever," Elvis said, and he was on his feet, an arm outstretched to help Grail up and they filed around tables and exited Starbucks, where Grail noted again that the rain suddenly stopped. He even saw the makings of a rainbow. They walked quickly down Pennsylvania Avenue to the Raddison, Elvis remembering more lines from Grail's book, but then abruptly shifting the conversation to his theories on the Shroud of Turin. When they reached the hotel Elvis nearly bounded through the door, but Grail hesitated, looked back for a moment, strangely aware he was looking to see if anyone had followed them. As he reached for the door handle it began to rain again, great cascades of it, the sun sprinting to the cover of clouds, and Grail had the nagging notion that it could not rain when Elvis was outside.

Chapter 16

▼

"Do you need a Cadillac, Grail?"

Elvis handed a Sierra Nevada pale ale to Grail from a cooler sent up by room service. Grail accepted the bottle, looked suspiciously at Elvis, a quick glance, but said nothing. He took a swig, a generous one. It was crackling cold and refreshing.

Elvis squirmed in his chair. They were seated side by side looking out the huge window of the presidential suite. The rain drummed hard against the window.

"What I mean is, would you like a Cadillac? Could you use one, Grail?"

Grail gulped down more beer. He turned toward Elvis, saw how earnest he was, the set jaw, the questioning, eager eyes. "What's this about a Cadillac?"

Elvis put his beer on the table next to him and then put his hands together as if about to pray.

"An El Dorado," Elvis said. "Or if you like, one of the new models. I can have one sent around just like that." He snapped his fingers for emphasis. "Would you like one, Grail? Could you use a Cadillac?"

"I already have a car."

"What kind, man? Do you already have a Cadillac?"

"No. I have a Passat. Back in Illinois."

"What kind of car is that, the Passat?"

"A Volkswagen. A forest green Volkswagen"

"I see. Forest green is a good color. So, you don't want a Cadillac? Is that what you're saying, Grail?"

Grail took another swig, nearly drained the bottle. "I guess not, Elvis."

"Call me E, if you like."

"Sure, E. How come you offered me a Cadillac?"

"Man, I just thought you might like one. No big deal. I used to get them for people."

They finished their beers silently and watched the rain. Elvis got up once and went to the bathroom. Grail remembered suddenly, sharply, that Elvis was once found nearly dead in his bathroom in Memphis from an overdose. Grail was relieved when he came back after a few minutes, but still he worried that fundamentally Elvis was quite insane. Or maybe he was just simple and generous to a fault. He seemed to remember hearing that Elvis used to give away Cadillacs and jewelry, often to strangers or people he felt needed help. Or maybe just to make himself feel good. Nothing wrong with that. Grail even began to feel titillated. It had sunk in: he was drinking beer with the king of rock and roll like they were buddies. Maybe they were. Insane or not, even Grail recognized cool when he saw it.

Elvis came to life again: "How are your parents, Grail? They still alive?"

"My mom teaches high school in Kalamazoo, Michigan." He felt a wall in his mind suddenly appear when he tried to articulate his father, that invisible man.

Elvis laughed, slapped a knee, laughed even harder and had to wipe spittle from his chin. "I'm sorry, man. Really." He laughed some more, softer. "Plenty of folks thought I was flipping burgers in Kalamazoo during the years when I didn't go out in public much. Hearing Kalamazoo just tickled me some."

Grail remembered from *National Enquirer* stories. "I'd quite forgotten that stuff, E. Pretty funny to think of it now."

Elvis composed himself, stared at the rain a moment. "You didn't say anything about your Pa. What about your Pa, Grail?"

"I never knew him," Grail said.

"No fooling? My daddy passed on a long time ago," Elvis said, his eyes cast toward the floor. "But I guess you know the details. Everybody knows the details. Yeah, man—part of being famous and all that."

Elvis fished two more beers out of the cooler. Getting drunk with Elvis Presley, Grail thought. Now that's one for the grandchildren if there ever are any.

"What are your regrets, Grail? Got any regrets?"

"You first, E. You're the king of rock and roll after all." Grail realized his tongue was a little loose form the beer. He wondered if Elvis would be offended.

Elvis laughed loudly, without inhibition. "Man, I stopped being the king a long time ago. But I'm OK with it. Really I am. I don't have that many regrets anymore, old son. Just my folks—just Vernon and Gladys. I loved them dearly. I almost died when they were both gone. But I came though it. I don't always know why I was spared. My wife, Betty Sue, she helped me a lot. I owe her a lot."

Grail was touched. He wished he could be as open. Well, Elvis was older, had been through so much more. Grail thought surely it gets easier with time, with experience.

"So, Grail, what do you regret, man?"

Grail thought hard. Feelings, real, honest feelings seemed sometimes to come hard. "Well, when I was a graduate student at Michigan, I was sort of dishonest. I do regret that. I—"

"You cheated?" Elvis frowned.

"Jesus, no. I never cheated as a student. I worked my ass off academically. That's not what I meant. I—"

"Either you cheated or you didn't."

"I didn't cheat. OK? I didn't cheat. Trust me. What I meant is I used to go around telling people I was a professor. But I wasn't. I was just a graduate assistant at the time. A teaching assistant. I wish I hadn't done it, but I did. I guess I was pretty full of myself, especially around women. If I met a nice woman I stretched things. I guess I didn't trust her to like me for who I was at the time."

"You did it to get girls," Elvis said. "Hey, I understand that. And you did become a professor, so case closed. But what about real regrets. You know, man, the big stuff."

"My father." Grail was surprised how easily it came out. He figured, finally, that it had been suppressed long enough the past few weeks and had to come out. "Like I said, I never knew him. Only recently did I find out he's alive, somewhere. I don't know where."

"Jesus, Grail. You mean you're telling me you just found out your pa is alive? After all these years? How long has it been, man? When did you find out?"

"A few weeks ago. My mom told me a few weeks ago. Pretty weird, eh?"

"Man, that's very weird." Elvis paced in front of the window. "Why did she wait so long? Why did she hide if from you all these years?"

"To protect me, of course. She found out he was a southern radical. He lied to her when he married her. She thought he was a regular guy. Even charming with his elaborate southern manners. But he hid everything—who he was. He hid the fact he belonged to the KKK and other radical groups. No offense, E. I mean, no offense to you as a southerner when I say he was radical."

"None taken, man." Elvis paced faster. "Would you like me to sing some gospel? I could sing something, maybe make you feel better about your pa."

"Sing? No, I don't think—"

"C'mon, Grail. It might make you feel better. How about a good church hymn?"

"Do you know one?"

"I know them all, man. I've sung them all, man."

Thanks, E, but I don't think so. I don't think a hymn is what I need. Maybe I don't need anything. It's OK. Really. I never knew my dad so there's not much to miss. Who he is now isn't my fault. It doesn't reflect on me. I won't let it."

"That's brave of you, Grail. But it has to eat at you some. Not knowing him, then hearing he's not how you'd like him to be."

Grail chewed on his lower lip, mulled it over a moment. "Maybe, but it'll be OK. I'll deal with it."

Elvis edged closer, was practically spilling out of his chair. "Are you going to find him, Grail? Shouldn't you go meet him, see what he's like at least?"

"I don't know, E. Some things are best left alone."

"Naw, man. You should find him. Really. Here, let's pray together." Elvis grabbed Grail's shoulder, the grip strong and commanding, and pulled him out of his chair onto his knees into the rich thick carpet, Grail nearly falling over, Elvis gripping him firmly around the waist, already launched into prayer, half aloud and half to himself, Grail not understanding all the words, feeling queasy, worried a housekeeper might suddenly come through the door and see them, but also faintly honored to pray on the floor of the presidential suite of the Confederate Plaza Radisson with the king of rock and roll.

Chapter 17

The man pulled up the collar of his raincoat, but it did little to keep the rain out. A damn umbrella, he thought. I should have brought a damn umbrella. A baseball cap wasn't enough. He backed deeper into the shadows under the green awning in front of the Eddie Bauer store and settled into the sweet spot where he was protected from the rain and mist. The shadows were comforting, enveloping.

He put a cigarette in his mouth, had the match lit, but thought better of it, worried it might draw attention. Be invisible, he reminded himself. Be a raindrop in the rain. Small. But he needed something to do, something in his hands. He fished a Jeb Stuart dollar coin from his pocket and bought a newspaper from a box near the Eddie Bauer door. Clots of customers scurried in and out, the rain no barrier to commerce. Good, the man thought. Very good. They make excellent cover.

Instinctively he pressed his back a little harder against the building when he spotted Elvis emerge from Starbucks across the street. Elvis lingered under the Starbucks awning, glanced at the sky with a moronic grin, but pulled his Bears cap tighter on his head. That's a nice touch, the man thought. The cap makes you just one of the people. A regular guy. Maybe even makes you look like an Elvis impersonator. The man smiled at the thought, then his focus tightened on Grail coming out the door. This was who he had come to see. Hudson looked across the street in his direction, but the man knew Grail would see only a shadowy figure at best, one of the many Washington citizens sheltering from the rain. Elvis tugged at Grail's coat sleeve and the two walked briskly toward the Radisson.

The man emerged slowly from the shelter of the awning. He again thought of an umbrella as he pulled the bill of his cap a little lower and slipped into the noisy stream of shoppers on his side of Virginia Avenue. Like the dozens of people surrounding him, the man looked up, saw that the rain had abruptly stopped. There was laughter and the metallic snaps of umbrellas closing almost in unison—like bayonets being fixed by soldiers, the man thought vaguely. Everyone seemed almost giddy over the sudden break. The man was indifferent, but remembered that the rain had also stopped when he first picked up Hudson and Elvis coming out of the Radisson. A curious thing.

Elvis was animated and gesturing wildly with his arms to Grail, who nodded his head and occasionally tried to get a word into the conversation. The man tracked them from his side of the avenue, careful to stay just behind them and out of the range of their peripheral vision. But it didn't really matter because Elvis was aware of little else but Elvis, and Grail seemed obsessed by his very presence. Grail seemed almost emotionless, the man observed. It was that way for blocks until they reached the Radisson, where Elvis virtually bounded through the door as Grail lingered, a hand on the handle and looking over his shoulder. For a moment the man thought he had been made and he lurched heavily to his left, but there was nowhere to hide and so he turned toward the nearest store window and pretended to shop. When he turned back Grail was gone. The man took a few steps toward the street, was debating whether to cross and go into the Radisson, but the rain was falling again, and he decided to stay put on his side of the street. He went into a Jeff Davis Chicken Hut and sat by the window.

Elvis Presley, he thought. Elvis the Pelvis. That was what they had called him years and years ago. Back when the man was a fresh-faced kid. When he was a teenager without a care in the world, just urges and abruptness and spontaneous fun. Back when he had headed north for a while, had left his country to find those greener pastures. After a while he decided there were no greener pastures. Just more pastures. One place is about as good as another, and moving around doesn't make much difference.

There had been a woman then. The beginning of a marriage. He had been a good-looking man in those days. Women noticed him. And then there was one that stood apart from the rest. She was smart. Too smart for him he finally realized—too late, perhaps. Was it really too late? No. No, nothing is too late. Everything just is or it isn't, and after, when it's all gone to hell, don't think of it in terms of too late or too anything—just realize it was and now it isn't. Simple as that. Don't dig deeper. There is no deeper. No greener pastures and no deeper.

Just…now, and then later there is something else. But always it's the same: things either are or they aren't. Black and white.

But he knew the factors. Politics had been one of the factors. At some point, back in those days, with that woman, he'd grown up some, got harder from his time in the industrialized U.S., and he'd felt what others felt, all the way back to The Cause: resentment at the U.S. for its ability to out produce everyone, to decide issues on the weight of numbers, the weight of products, the weight of…the weight…and now, an old man, he was tired.

Where was he? Oh, yes—Elvis. He had been musing about Elvis before the unexpected and unwelcome return to the past. Yes, the now—keep with the now and forget the then. There are no greener pastures and no deeper anything. Remember that. So, let's see—yes, Elvis. Still the comical figure. He had heard Elvis was in the capital and he was awfully surprised to see him with Grail. He had not expected anything of the sort. Interesting. Elvis and Grail Hudson. What was the connection? No greener pastures, no deeper. Remember that. But then the man finally allowed himself to think of Grail as more than just a figure walking beside Elvis and he knew: yes, there is deeper, and it's a terrible place. And I will have to go there.

He pondered that a while, then felt hunger creep over him. He picked up a menu, but wasn't really sure what he wanted. Maybe some soup to warm him up. He looked up once and gazed out at the avenue. It was getting late, the sky darkening, and there was a pelting rain as the relentless shoppers churned the avenue under a sea of umbrellas.

Across the street a young woman emerged slowly from under an awning in front of Sak's and opened her umbrella. She stole a glance at the man as he sat by the window and pored over a menu. He looked out the window once, in her direction, but she knew he would not notice anything out of the ordinary. Just another fashionably dressed young woman on the avenue. She produced a cell phone and turned away, saying softly, "We have company."

Chapter 18

Grail basked in the cosmic glow that came from being a satellite orbiting the leviathan planet Elvis. Leslie Sheridan sat opposite him at a table by the window of his room at the Raddison. She couldn't think of how to sugarcoat her message, so she brushed bangs of hair away from her face and said it flat out: "You're being followed—watched, whatever."

It didn't sink in at first. His face was slow to show emotion. Followed? How strange. Followed? As in secret agents? Like something out of *The Ipcress File?* Or a Hitchcock film? He gaped at Leslie, giving her a few stomach butterflies, although she wasn't sure why, and then he arched his eyebrows and allowed a small frown to appear.

"Followed?"

She eased back in her chair and watched him. He was handsome—boyish, really—and she liked that in someone who was obviously a brilliant academic. She wondered, though, how much common sense does the man possess? That was important, too. And there was more to tell him. Much more. This was just the introductory stuff. She wondered how he would handle it when she got to the real reason for her visit. And of course then there was the ball. The pain in the ass reunification ball, where they had to juggle Elvis and Hudson—and, oh, yes, Mr. Porno, Wad Upshot, and countless other guests. My God, President Clinton would be there. President Carter. Yoko Ono for Christ's sake.

"I'm being watched?" she heard him say, though it seemed far away, or perhaps under water. He looked like he thought it a joke he was slow to getting. He tried to manage a grin, but it was not authentic, stemmed from a fundamental disbelief that it was the right way to go.

"By who, Leslie? Who is watching me?"

"There's a dissident group," she said. "It's small."

It still had not sunk in totally for him, had still not gone from data to realization in his mind. "Really?"

Leslie wondered if he was slow. Could he leap with quicksilver speed in the world of books, but be merely a plodder in real life, unable to connect the dots in time to avoid a bus bearing down on him?

"Yes," she said quietly. "Really."

"Ok," he said, but still shaky, still not connected to it all yet, still thinking surely a punch line was coming. "So, what do you mean by dissident? Why would they be interested in me? I'm just a history teacher."

She leaned forward, then felt self-conscious for appearing to be secretive, so she eased back, put her palms flat on the table. "They're anti-reunification, Dr. Hudson. People who don't want the union back. Remember the bomb in Dupont Circle? We're confident they were behind it."

Grail got up and went to the window. The rain was softer, barely there—almost not raining at all, and he wondered vaguely if that meant Elvis was back on the streets.

"It's a mistake," he said, still looking out the window. "It's Elvis, right? They're following Elvis. I was with him all day yesterday."

"No," she said. "We don't believe they are interested in Elvis one way or another."

He turned back toward her. "It has to be Elvis. Really, who would follow *me*?"

She looked away, smoothed her dress. "More people than would follow Elvis, I'm afraid."

He studied her face, liked it very much. Then it hit him. "Wait a second," he said.

"Wait a damn minute—how do you *know* someone is following me?"

His eyes began to bore through her and she fidgeted, finally had to bolt out of her chair and walk around the room.

"Leslie?"

"We know that because we're following you, too. Sorry, but that's the reality of it."

"I'm being followed by the CSA? Whose idea was that?"

"State," she said. "Finch. Although Attorney General Dashcroft probably was in on it, too. He wants everyone followed. Anyway, Finch wanted to guarantee your safety. In the process our people discovered you were being tailed by somebody else."

"Oh, it's for my protection," he said, his voice rising, indignant, but also still a little baffled by it all.

"Of course," she said. "You're a guest of the CSA—a VIP. We can't have you in danger, you know."

"Am I in danger?" He wondered about that suddenly. It had never occurred to him before. Because of what he wrote about Lee? Could it be over that? Some misguided hillbilly rebel afraid reunification dooms the Confederacy and is looking for a fat target?

"It's always a possibility in these affairs," she said, realizing she sounded detached, official. "But security teams are in place."

"Elvis, too"

"Yes, Elvis, too. But do you think he'll even notice?"

Grail smiled. "He knows more than he lets on. I found that out. He's crafty."

"I can't wait to see him tomorrow at the ball," she said. "Love Me Tender will somehow sound surreal to me as the unofficial theme for reunification. Are the USA and CSA really like two lovers ready to give it a second go around?"

Grail shrugged. "It might be that simple. I don't know. Hey, I missed reunification altogether. I guess I was so consumed with my own little world I forgot to watch for the signs. I don't know, Leslie. Maybe so. Maybe it will be a smooth reunion. But those dissidents, as you call them, are troublesome. They worry me. How far will they go? How long will they pursue it?"

"There's only been the one bomb," she said. "And no one has been killed. Maybe they will make their pathetic gestures and then slink away. Maybe crawl back under whatever rocks they oozed from under in the first place." She was stalling, but he didn't seem to notice, was obviously lost in thought. She wished she could just leave, leave the task up to someone else. But there wasn't anyone else. And to sidestep it would just mark her as weak in Finch's eyes.

"Dr. Hudson, there's something else. I need to tell you something. I—"

"Call me Grail. Please. All that Dr. Hudson stuff makes me seem old—like an old white-headed academic."

"Of course," she said. "Grail." She sensed he was flirting with her very subtlely. She found that she didn't mind. Maybe even liked the attention from him. How old was he? Forty-three?

"I sure hope you're not going to tell me I have to make some speech tonight. Good Lord, I'd like to just sit on the sidelines and take it all in."

"No, there's no speech. Don't worry about that. But I'm afraid I haven't told you all I know about who's following you."

She had a grave look on her face, and he wondered, what is coming? What have I missed? "Go ahead, Leslie. Just say it. You seem pretty good at that."

She went to the window and looked out for a moment. The rain was still there, was always there, but it had for some time seemed to be easing. She felt him come up near her, just over her shoulder.

"What is it, Leslie?"

She turned and they were close. Too close for such a moment, she felt. But the look on his face was serious and not full of romantic notions. Why did that occur to her at a timelike this? She looked closer, saw he was a little scared.

"The man who followed you—we've identified him."

"Who is he?"

"Your father, Grail. Lewis Hudson."

"Oh," he said quietly. Grail looked in her eyes for a long moment, then turned away, toward the window. She watched as he looked out the window and ran a hand through his thick hair. "Confirmed?" he finally said, without looking at her. "Your people are sure? There's no mistake?" His tone carried a note of resignation, as though something he had long suspected was finally in the open.

"No mistake."

He sat on the edge of the bed and glanced up at her, his eyebrows arched in that subtle way that she found boyish and endearing. But this was not the time for that.

"Are you OK, Grail?"

"I don't know. I don't know how I'm supposed to feel. Believe me, since finding out my father is alive, I have never quite known what to feel, or do. Do you suppose there's something I should actually do? Is there a manual for people who discover their fathers are terrorists?"

"I wish there was," she said. "I'd buy you one."

"Would you, Leslie?"

"Of course."

Grail looked away. "Is he really a terrorist? Is he going to be arrested?"

"I don't know," she said. "They're trying to assess his involvement. That's what I'm told. I know it's not much. Sorry."

She watched his face for a clue on how to help him, but saw only the wrinkles of confusion and frustration. Still, she could see—sense was a better way to put it—that he really did want an answer, really did desperately want to know something. "I'm not sure what to say."

"Join the club." There really wasn't so much to say, though, he admitted to himself. Sure, he thought, he's my father. Lewis Hudson. That's a technical thing. Blood. One of those things nobody has control over. But I have never met the man and I am now in my 40s. How should I view him? He's a stranger. Is he a terrorist, too? Maybe. That's worth looking into, to see just who he is and who he is associated with. But father? Not really. Of course, it's not so simple as all that, but for now it's all I can come up with. Jesus H. Christ. He reached across the bed and grabbed his jacket. "I could stand a drink. How about you? I've been dying to check out the Gettysburg Lounge downstairs."

She wasn't sure it was a good idea, and she hesitated, analyzing it too much, but finally said, "Why not?"

"Good," he said. "For a moment there you had a funny look on your face. Everything OK?"

"I'm fine," she said, feeling a little self-conscious that he picked up on her uncertainty.

"I was just thinking I should be asking how *you* are."

He opened the door for her. "Well, I'm working on that, Leslie."

"We'll work on it together," she said. "Deal?"

"Deal."

The walls and even the ceiling of the Gettysburg Lounge were covered in murals depicting various stages of the Confederate defeat at Gettysburg. Grail quickly spotted Lee, Longstreet, and Pickett. Pickett's charge was beautifully done and quite historically accurate. The loss of life had been appalling and there it was true to life, but Grail thought that surely the choice of subject must eventually wear on the lounge's patrons, especially those who had had too much to drink. He thought the victories at Chancellorsville or Fredericksburg would have made for a happier atmosphere for CSA drinkers. The names seemed awfully compatible: Fredericksburg Lounge. Chancellorsville Lounge. He especially liked the regal sound associated with Chancellorsville Lounge.

"These murals are magnificent," he said. "But also pretty damn depressing."

Leslie nodded, but said nothing. She was enjoying how Grail seemed like a little kid discovering a local museum for the first time.

"I'm curious," Grail said to the bartender. "Does anyone ever feel a little oppressed that all this stuff essentially depicts a Confederate loss?"

"Only folks from the USA tend to look at it that way," the bartender said, but he quickly smiled so as not to appear too insolent. "Actually, we like to have Gettysburg around as a reminder of how we almost lost the war. It's good to remember that."

"I suppose," Grail said, not sure if he should feel offended or just let it go. They are such a nationalist bunch, these Confederates. Yes, that' what they still are: Confederates. Well over a hundred years as an actual by God country and they are still rebels to the core, still full of a sense of drama and catharsis and an unshakeable belief in their destiny. The United States, he began to sense, was something quite different. Living in his ivory tower in Illinois he had become too insulated to what was really all around him. He had for a very long time neglected to see the USA as too capitalist, too concerned with material wealth. A country without a compelling and noble national goal. Make more money? Not very noble, though compelling to far too many politicians and corporatists. The CSA, he began to understand, had something else: pride. The north just had smaller and smaller cell phones and bigger and bigger SUVs.

Leslie clinked her glass against his. "Let's toast something. Here we are in this nice bar, with these gorgeous murals, drinking southern bourbon, and we haven't toasted anything."

"All right," Grail said, clinking his glass against hers. "But what? Who?"

"Robert E. Lee?"

"Very funny. Will cameras suddenly burst in to catch me toasting the guy I keep dumping on?"

"Nope. You're safe."

"Sure I am, now that your security folks are on the job. Your gray ghosts, I guess." There was a trace of resentment in his voice and he regretted it. "I didn't mean anything by that. The bourbon is beginning to speak a little."

"It's OK," she said. "I'd be a little jumpy in your place."

He glanced around, studied the faces of several young men in suits at the end of the bar. "Any of them in here?" He inspected the two men closer, looked at their coats to see if he might detect the bulge of a gun. "What about those two? Down at the end of the bar." Grail lifted his drink and nodded their way, but the men ignored him.

Leslie squeezed his elbow gently and leaned closer. "Not so loud. If any of them are here I won't know them. The idea is for no one to know who they are."

"Right," he said. "Sorry. Did I speak too loud?"

"You didn't, but your bourbon might have raised its voice a tad."

"Well, I guess I'm feeling it some."

"What's this about gray ghosts?" she said.

"It just came to me. Some stealthy Confederate officer was nicknamed the Gray Ghost. Can't remember his damn name, though."

"Are you getting drunk, Grail?"

"No, not drunk. Just buzzed a little."

She sipped her drink and then chuckled softly. "Me, too. So what do you think Elvis is doing right now? The King. Did you like him when you were a kid?"

"I don't know." Grail mulled it over. "I guess I did. I remember seeing some of his movies on TV a few times. Yeah, I guess I did like him, but I didn't think much about him at the time. It's weird to be his buddy. I think that's what I am now, his sidekick. But who knows how long that will last."

"Nothing lasts forever," Leslie said. She downed her drink. "I've got to run. Too many things to do for the ball."

"It's been a long day. Why not have one more drink and keep me company."

"I can't, Grail. It would be fun, but duty calls."

"Ah, duty," he said, downing his own drink. "Duty plays pretty big down here."

"It's practically our motto," she said. "You'll manage. You're a big boy, right?"

"If you say so."

"You're in good hands—you know that, Grail."

"That's true. I just don't know whose hands to look for."

"You'll meet your guardian angels tomorrow when they pick you up for the ball. Good night, Grail."

He waved to her as she paused at the door.

"Don't forget your tux," she called. "I bet you'll look like James Bond."

"How appropriate. See you tomorrow."

Grail had one more drink and then went to his room. On the way up in the elevator a man read the Washington Post without looking up. At Grail's floor the man stayed in the car but looked up with a faint smile and wished him a good evening. The door closed before Grail could say anything. So, the gray ghosts had faces after all.

It had been a while. Grail was slow to embrace the dream, to go from absolute reality to a place he had long thought to be another type of reality, one accessible only in sleep. Not merely a dream as many thought of dreams, but a plane of existence, perhaps even governed by the concept of leaving the physical body. A prelude to heaven? An intermediate location.

It came in spurts, then was clear and continous. Lee waved to him, almost as though waving to an old friend—maybe Longstreet, or Stonewall Jackson.

"You're well?" Lee said. "We haven't talked in quite a spell."

Grail studied the general, who for the first time was dressed in the ornate new uniform he had worn when the war ended and he received Grant. The Lee of history books. The Lee that made Grant seem a shabby teamster instead of general.

"I'm OK," Grail said. "The uniform is something. I'm impressed."

"It seemed appropriate, given the fact you are in the CSA. Of course, what I wear—"

"I know, I know," Grail said. "I make the rules and decide what you wear. It's my dream, right?"

Lee smiled, a full smile with gleaming teeth. "You're catching on. I think you might have made a decent member of my staff. Perhaps a major."

"Well, why not?" Grail said. "Now that I know I am descended from a Confederate officer."

"Littlefield Hudson troubles you?" Lee frowned.

"No. He was a good man. At least from what I know. He turned away from you, though, and the Confederacy. Did you know that?"

"We don't get the papers up here. Or television. But information filters down to us nonetheless. It's OK. Littlefield and I see each other sometimes."

"Over checkers?"

"That's right," Lee said. "Sometimes Grant and Longstreet come to watch. Grant needles Littlefield about capturing Lincoln and preventing him from finishing us off. But it's friendly stuff. Everyone gets along."

"Do you see any of the slaves up there?"

Lee smiled again. "Everyone is here. Everybody sees everybody else. I see Lincoln from time to time. He and Jeff Davis have these arguments that are quite something to witness I might tell you."

"I can imagine," Grail said. "Listen, don't be offended, but I asked about the slaves for a reason: you were a racist. It was subtle enough. But it was there. It was in some of your letters. I read them."

"True enough. You are right, my young friend. Things change once you get here. If they don't you get transferred to a warmer climate."

"How? How do they change?"

Lee shifted in his imaginary chair on air. "That's a tough one."

"As tough as the choices you made at Gettysburg?"

"Much tougher," Lee said. "But the remark was unkind."

"Sorry. It just slipped out."

"That's fine. We're pretty big on forgiveness around here."

"Then you'll tell me how it works up there?"

"I can't. You don't have the clearance for that. In time, my boy. In time. Some things must remain secret for a while. Wait and see. I changed. It's inevitable. But you are troubled. What troubles you?"

Grail tried to think. It was hard. What were his fears? It was just really hard to get them into something like words or thoughts or anything at all that would give them a sense of concept. There were currents of feelings and rumblings, things coming in and out of focus, and all the time a sort of creeping dread that most of the time he caught only glimmers of, but sometimes could feel like a shroud. Did any of that make sense? Lee watched him with a great air of benevolence about him.

"We walk around lost, pretending to know where we are going," finally tumbled out of Grail's mouth. "We fear death but rush toward it without trying to know what it means."

"It doesn't mean what many of you think it does," Lee said.

"I don't know what I think it means," Grail said. "But I do fear it."

"I did, too. What else do you fear?"

Grail hesitated, but knew the answer right away: "The hollow place I sometimes feel inside. That place where doubt comes from. The place inside me that sometimes screams, what should I do?"

"Do you have an answer for it?"

"No. Do you?"

"Yes," Lee said. "Of course. Up here all that becomes clear. But I can't—"

"Gotcha," Grail said. "I probably don't have the clearance for that."

Lee smiled the generous smile a good father would give his son. "If it's any consolation, I predict you will fill the hollow place."

"I wish I could be so sure," Grail said. "I have such doubts sometimes. I don't know who I am sometimes. Sometimes I wonder, what has my life added up to so far? I just don't know."

"An opportunity is before you, son. You just have to recognize it and accept the challenge. Your salvation is there."

"Does it concern my father?"

"We have many fathers," Lee said, and abruptly his image dissolved.

Grail found himself hurtling along a dark corridor, but he could see, though he could not articulate the concept of sight, could not articulate anything on a language level. He just *was*, and hurtling. But it was comfortable and it went on for what seemed an eternity, and then when it was morning his body was awake and propped up against the pillows before his mind had made the transfer from one reality to the other. He could not keep his eyes open at first. They fluttered, allowing brief images in from around his room: a shadow on the wall that at first he thought might be a giant letter T, the dark and strange symbol of his father, of Lewis Hudson, but just as quickly he recognized there were to be no more letter Ts. It was a feeling. An irrefutable feeling accompanied by a sense of well-being that quickly evaporated, but he knew—no, he felt—could be tapped into again. When his eyes did finally slowly focus they rested on the plump recliner in a corner of the room.

In it sat a smiling Elvis.

Chapter 19

"A maid let me in," Elvis said as though it made perfect sense. "All it took was an autograph."

Grail's eyes had finally focused and he had accepted it was really Elvis and not part of the dream. He sat up, a mild hangover headache kicking in, his throat a little raw.

"Great," Grail said, blinking. "I need some water."

"No problem, man." Elvis bounded toward the bathroom and came back with a glass of water.

"Much better," Grail said. "What time is it?"

"Nearly eleven," Elvis said, checking his watch. "What time did you go to bed?"

"Not too late. I had a few drinks in the lounge last night. Maybe more than I should have, I guess." Grail slid off the bed into a sitting position on an edge of the mattress. He rubbed his head and yawned. "How long have you been sitting there?"

"Only a few minutes. I just got back from a walk after breakfast. They serve some mean hash browns and biscuits and gravy downstairs."

"*Why* were you sitting there?" Grail said, but he realized that somehow it was just no big deal to wake up to Elvis Presley watching him and fetching water. It just seemed sort of natural these days. Right up there with discovering his father might be a terrorist. This was one he'd have to tell Darla about. He got up and looked out the window. It took a few moments for him to realize the sun was peeking from behind fading clouds and there was no rain. He glanced quickly back at Elvis, but before Elvis could explain his presence, Grail muttered, "When did it stop?" He looked out again, half expecting to be mistaken. "When did it quit raining?"

"Around dawn," Elvis said.

"Were you up then?"

"Yes, I was," Elvis said. "I used to be a night owl and sleep all day, but these days I get up with the birds."

Grail got more water from the bathroom. "Well, my friend, there's some symbolism here, that's for sure. People were worried the CSA might just float away and now the rain has finally stopped—on the day of the damn reunification ball. Some heavy duty symbolism."

"It can't rain forever," Elvis said as he shrugged his shoulders.

Then a realization abruptly flooded Grail's brain. "All you had to do to get in was bribe a housekeeper?"

"Yeah, man. Nice lady. She said she saw me in Vegas back in the old days."

Grail stared at Elvis a moment. "What about the security we're supposed to have around here?"

"They're around," Elvis said. "That's who I had breakfast with this morning. There's a guy at the end of the hall right now."

"Hallelujah," Grail said. "I'm going to take a shower."

"I'll be right here," Elvis said happily. "I'm re-reading your book." He grabbed it off the floor and held it up, but Grail had already closed the door.

Elvis invited Grail to ride in his limo to the ball. In the elevator on the way down Grail took in the spectacle of Elvis's tux: shimmering gold with wide lapels and tails. Rhinestone rubies and emeralds sprinkled generously down the front. He wielded a jewel-encrusted baton. Grail wore a traditional black tux, a la James Bond, that he thought made him look even a little dashing in the mirror in his room.

"Where do you get something like that?" Grail said. "Do they have those at a mall?"

"I have a guy that makes my stuff. I designed this one myself."

"Real jewels on that baton?"

"Yeah, man. Real as it gets. You want to carry it a while?" He gave it to Grail, who was surprised at how heavy it was. The diamonds sparkled under the elevator lights.

"Incredible," Grail said as he handed it back. "But too rich for my blood. I'd feel vaguely like Herman Goering."

Elvis thought about that a second. "Oh, yeah."

CSA State Department agents escorted them out a backdoor of the Radisson into the limo. One of the agents climbed in the front seat with the driver, who also was from State. It was nearly dark as the limo pulled away from the curb onto Virginia Avenue.

"I guess you don't want a drink, not after this morning," Elvis said, pointing to the well-stocked limo bar.

"Pass," Grail said." Maybe a glass of champagne at the big wingding."

"It's going to be a good one," Elvis said. "A real wingding."

"And you're going to sing."

"Yes, sir—I am. Looking forward to the honor."

"I forget what you're singing."

"Love Me Tender. Special request from President Carter."

"Ah. Well, that's a good one."

Elvis was suddenly intrigued and leaned closer to Grail who sat opposite him. "Was it your favorite, Grail? Can I have the pleasure of it being one you especially liked?" Elvis looked awfully hopeful, like a kid thinking there was a new bike about to appear under his Christmas tree.

"I liked it, E. Everybody did, I guess."

"It wasn't your favorite? Is that what you're saying, Grail?" Elvis was slowly pulling back.

Grail had to think hard and fast. He didn't really know the Elvis musical catalogue, just a few tunes from the movies. "Well, now I did like that other one—Return To Sender. Yeah, E, maybe that's my favorite."

Elvis was still frowning a little. "You're saying you don't know which one's your favorite?"

"Not at all. Return to Sender's the one. I always liked that one."

Satisfied, Elvis sat back and smiled. "Me, too. I always get a kick out of that one."

They sat and smiled at each other for what seemed to Grail like a long time. He wondered if Elvis was slipping into one of those little moments where reality was a concept too high up for him to reach when Elvis suddenly leaned forward and reached over Grail's shoulder to tap on the glass partition. Realizing his mistake he picked up the inter-phone and asked the driver to pull over as soon as he could.

"What's up?" Grail looked out the windows but saw only blackness.

"I've been thinking," Elvis said.

Grail immediately sensed the danger in that. "What's wrong? Why are we stopping?"

Elvis seemed to be encouraging a thought to finally depart his brain and shoot out his mouth. "Your pa. I've been thinking about your pa, and I think we should go find him. before these CSA boys do."

Grail stared, felt a surprising sliver of anger. "You can't be serious?"

"Sure I am. I've been thinking hard on it. He's your pa and you don't know him. My pa is long dead. I miss him all the time. But he's not ever coming back to see me. You can still see yours."

"Why would I want to see mine? He's a terrorist. Or a wannabe terrorist. Either way he doesn't sound like father of the year material."

"It might not be that simple," Elvis said. "At breakfast those CSA boys told me your pa seems to be on the fringe of things. No real evidence linking him to that bomb that went off."

"You mean he's just pals with terrorists, but just not officially one of them," Grail said sarcastically. "Sort of like a guy who brings them milk and brownies in between raids?" A moment later Grail said. "Or even sort of like Archie Bunker." Grail thought, how odd to suddenly think of an episode of "All in the Family.

"Archie Bunker?" Elvis looked amused. "Man, you've lost me on that one."

"You don't know who Archie Bunker is, E?"

"Sure I do. From TV, man. I loved that show, but what's it got to do with this?"

"I know it's weird to think of that suddenly, but I recall what Lionel said—you remember Lionel, right, the black kid who lived next door to the Bunkers?"

"Sure."

"Well, Lionel once said that Archie probably wouldn't burn a cross in anybody's yard, but he might roast a weiner at one—something like that."

"Yeah, I do remember that one," Elvis said. "That was a funny one."

"Maybe that's how my father would be," Grail said. "I don't know. Pretty weird to think of Archie Bunker at a time like this. I'm just trying to make sense of all this, where my father might fit in—who the bastard is."

"They aren't exactly sure where he fits in, Grail, but it could be what you say, sort of. That he's friends with some folks that are the real bad ones."

"That's a fairy tale, E. No offense."

"None taken, man. But you don't know the South, my friend. Oh, you know the history of the CSA, the historical stuff that's far-reaching and all that, but you don't know Southern people. They recall what it meant to go to war to make a country. Some of them see reunification as the end of the CSA—a giving into the union just as though Grant had won and the Confederacy was drug back to it."

Grail admitted to himself that he didn't really know that, could never know that growing up in Michigan and teaching in Illinois. Elvis was right. It wasn't something you could know very well at all without knowing Southerners, without living among them. The rebels just never gave up. Even after so many years as a nation. They had something the North could never have, he supposed. A sense of more than just pride. A sense of mission. It was flawed, to be sure, but it was a mission. It was something more than just the ugly obsession with making more and more money like in the United States. The CSA always wanted to suppress industrialization and the pitfalls of unfettered capitalism. It had prospered, too, but in its own way. Massive profit was scorned. Instead, the corporations of the CSA are actually regulated and forced to be good corporate citizens, to respect the environment, and to look at more than jut a balance sheet as indicators of corporate health. In the CSA executives can be jailed for stealing from their employees. Secret loans at low interest rates to buy stock are a serious offense in the CSA. That's why the former governor of Texas, George W. Bush, finally emigrated to the United States, where sweetheart corporate deals are just business as usual and the notion of punishing executives who plunder and pillage is a joke.

"Hey," Elvis said. "You still with me, Grail?"

Grail blinked a few times. "Sorry, I was thinking."

"I reckon so. You look like you just transported your brain to the Bahamas."

"Texas, actually. Listen, E, there's a hole in your theory. If my father is just a...groupie for terrorists, for lack of a better phrase—"

"Groupie." Elvis slapped his knee. "That's a good one. I like that."

"Right. Well, if he's just a groupie, why would the CSA be watching him so close? And better yet, why did he come to Washington and follow us?"

"He didn't follow us," Elvis said. "He followed *you*. As much as I love my fans I don't think he's one of them. He was watching *you*. That's what the CSA boys say. Look, they're just doing their job and taking into account the possibilities."

"What *are* possibilities?" Grail felt he had to be sold a little more, but he was leaning toward what Elvis was saying.

"Well, that you pa is or isn't a terrorist. Those are the possibilities. He is one, or he just knows them, and they're trying to find out. His coming to town, you have to admit, would naturally get their attention."

"I guess," Grail said. "What are you proposing we do about all this?"

"We find him, Grail. We go find him and maybe we stop some tragedy from coming down the road."

Grail regarded the serious look on Elvis's face, the set jaw and conviction in his eyes. "What do you get out of this, E? Why do you care? Why do you want to do this?"

Elvis fingered the massive baton and looked out the window at the blackness for a moment. "Like I said, my pa is gone. Maybe yours is still worth something. If so, it would make me feel good to be there at the end, when all that comes down."

"Just to feel good, E? Is it that simple?"

"Sure it is, man. That's the lesson I learned. Nearly died before I learned it, too. Sure, I still have jewels and limos and stuff, but I've learned those are just toys. Hell, I know what I look like in the getup. But people sort of expect it from me. Anyway, what really counts is doing things you can feel good about because you know you helped someone else. Lord knows that's why I gave people Cadillacs and such when I was young. For a long time after I was young I was lost and forgot about that, but I made my way back to it."

Grail mulled it over. One of the State agents came over the inter-phone and reminded Elvis they were running late for the ball.

"Yeah, man, "Elvis said into the phone. "Let's go. We're ready."

"Are we?" Grail said.

"Well," Elvis said, "if we're not, then we'll sure know it soon enough."

The limo lurched forward. Grail, too felt he had been thrown into gear and a direction, but a direction down a long dark lane toward deeper blackness with no promise of light.

Part III

Chapter 20

Robert, who had arrived in a battered taxi with a noisy muffler, watched from a balcony as Elvis and Grail exited their limo to a dignitary's welcome at Great Confederate Hall. A band played "Dixie" as cameras flashed and a legion of Elvis fans surged against security teams lining the hall entrance. Daughters of the Confederacy gave Elvis and Grail roses, then linked arms with them for the walk into the hall, where rose petals were scattered in their path.

Robert had been greeted at a side entrance by a young State flunky who explained the lack of a limo must have been an oversight. The man had vanished after they were inside and Robert knew he was on his own. His invitation was purely a reluctant courtesy to see what public relations mileage might be had from a reformed porn star graciously and compassionately admitted to the CSA to visit a dying brother. It had become the season for anyone desiring to be welcomed back into the fold.

Once inside the dome of the Great Hall Robert was astonished when he looked up: it seemed room enough for a squadron of helicopters to maneuver. Nothing he had heard or read about it could have prepared him. He had entered a palace only gods could fill. Indeed, suspended around the dome's interior and lit by floodlights were 250-foot banners of the legends of the Confederacy: Lee, Jackson, Longstreet, Beauregard, and Davis. The CSA's Mt. Rushmore.

Only after a few more steps was he aware of people, many hundreds of men and women in elegant tuxedos and flowing gowns, some already dancing, but most in clumps and knots of animated conversation. Robert could not keep his eyes from wandering up, but soon he sensed someone near and getting nearer. Then a man's soft voice.

"It's almost 1,000 feet to the skylight turret," Mallory Wade said. "The cost was staggering, and sometimes it makes me uneasy, as though it's something that might have been created at Nuremberg, if you get my meaning."

Robert looked up again. "I know what you mean. It has that same scope."

"But the people adore it," Mallory said. "And for that reason alone it's worth every penny."

Robert nodded. "Put down some grass and the Redskins could play games here. No chance the punter would ever hit the ceiling."

Wade offered his hand. "You're Robert Whitfield, of course. I'm Mallory Wade."

"Thanks for the invitation, Mr. Wade."

"You are a Virginian, sir, and therefore welcome."

"Frankly, I didn't expect it," Robert said, figuring he might as well break the porno ice first to get it out of the way. "I may be a Virginian, but I figured my…youthful indiscretions would prevent me from ever attending an event like this."

Wade thought about Robert's exploits, the few he had seen anyway, and had to work hard to suppress a grin. He suspected that Robert knew what he was thinking.

"Well, Mr. Whitfield, you won't be running for Congress any time soon, but otherwise reunification makes many things possible. It's a new beginning for everyone. Care for some champagne?"

"I could stand some."

Mallory led Robert to the bar, past the Stars and Bars and Old Glory, each measuring 200 feet by 200 feet, hanging side by side behind the dais that would embrace Presidents Carter, Clinton, and other VIPs.

"Equally staggering is the champagne bill," Mallory said. "Dom Perignon."

"But it makes the people happy, right?"

"Very happy, Mr. Whitfield."

"Robert."

"Robert," Mallory said, but he thought: Wad Upshot. It would take some time before that automatic image would fade. "Please, call me Mallory—or Mal."

"OK, Mal. Listen, I don't mean to be blunt, but we do have a friend in common—Mr. Gordon from *People* magazine? He has spoken to you, right? We have an arrangement?"

"Let's step over here, out of the line of fire," Mallory said, steering Robert by the arm away from the bar toward a hallway. Several young women recognized

Robert. One of them finally summoned the courage and dashed over for an autograph. Robert signed it with his real name, which disappointed her.

"Just this once?" she said.

"Sorry, but Wad is no more. That's the past."

"That was some past," she said. "If Wad decides to come back, here's my phone number."

Robert was polite and the woman was attractive, tempting, but knew he would throw the number away. He just couldn't go back to those days. Reunification, he knew, was the door swinging open, the event so large that he could ride its coattails and reinvent himself. All he needed was the right angle. He figured that angle had to somehow be connected to Elvis. It was as likely a possibility as anything else he had so far considered.

"Now then," Mallory said, looking around to make sure they were alone. "I did speak with Mr. Gordon."

"Good," Robert said. He was eager. "He agreed to interview you for the magazine?"

"He did." Mallory lowered his voice. "It's an excellent opportunity for me."

"Of course it is," Robert said. He sipped the champagne and started to relax, to think it was becoming fun to make the deal, to begin the task of reinventing himself. "You'll come off as one of the prime movers and shakers in this whole shindig. Maybe a promotion. Or a political career. Senator Wade has a good ring to it. Have you thought about that?"

Mallory admitted to himself that he had not, but the idea suddenly amazed him. It sat well with his ambition.

"Let's drink to that, Mal—your future."

Mallory raised his glass. "Thanks, Robert. It's gracious of you." Mallory was beginning to let his inhibitions slip away, to not worry about what Finch might think when he appeared in *People*. To hell with Finch. By then it would be too late. By then he would be indentified with reunification in so profound a way as to launch him in the public's mind. He would become more than just a State messenger boy. A political career? Senator Wade? Why not? The article would give him visibility and credibility. His family connections would then kick in and provide a political base, money. There was something to it. He was sure. And to think he might owe the start of it to a retired porn star. Yes, reunification did indeed make many things possible.

Robert grabbed two more glasses of champagne and handed one to Mallory. Then he gripped Mallory's shoulder and focused his eyes on Mallory's. "Now,

Mal, there's just the rest of the bargain to hammer out—that introduction to Elvis. I saw him arrive a little while ago."

Mallory snapped back into the moment, his lovely fantasy of the future temporarily shelved. He blinked several times. "Elvis. Yes—Elvis. Of course."

Robert gripped Mallory's shoulder firmly. "You can do it, right? A one-on-one meeting?"

For a moment fantasy returned and Mallory saw himself as Senator Wade, able to do anything at all, by God and General Jackson. "Don't worry, Robert. It's as good as done. I'm going to greet Elvis now. I'll send someone for you when it's time, so be patient."

Mallory started off, stopped, and faced Robert. "Why is it so important that you meet Elvis? I've wondered about that. What's in it for you?"

"The soothing calm of perspective, Mal. When a man is starting over he needs perspective. Don't you agree?"

Mallory pondered that a moment, but quickly became Senator Wade again and moved light years beyond perspective. "Why, yes. Of course. I won't be long. A half hour." He scurried away with an imperial air.

"Don't forget me, Mal," Robert called after him. He downed the remainder of his champagne and thrust his hands in his pockets, abruptly a little gloomy, a little nervous, fully aware that he had not the slightest idea yet why he wanted to meet Elvis, only that he had perhaps a half hour to figure it out.

Elvis glided through the hall as though mounted on wheels. The graying, portly buddha of rock and roll had summoned up the old sneer and swagger and cut through the crowd of admirers with an amused Grail trailing in his wake. Women still swooned. Men still grinned in fascination and wanted to shake his hand. Even Yoko Ono was speechless as Elvis swept past her like a glittering frigate under golden sail.

President Clinton embraced Elvis with a bear hug. President Carter, a little intimidated by the display of emotion, settled for a warm handshake. Both presidents posed for pictures with an arm around Elvis's considerable waist. Elvis called Grail over and the four posed for a picture that would appear on the cover of *Life*. The presidents then adjourned for a private chat and Mallory guided Elvis and Grail to a hall of dressing rooms behind the dais. In half an hour Elvis would sing "Love me Tender" and then Clinton and Carter would sign papers making the CSA and USA officially one united nation again.

Mallory had champagne delivered to Elvis and Grail. A few minutes later he delivered a nervous Robert Whitfield to the dressing room.

"Have a seat, man." Elvis pointed to a plush black leather recliner identical to the two he and Grail were immersed in.

"Thanks, Mr. Presley."

"Call me E, if you like. This is Dr. Grail Hudson, my friend."

"Just Grail," Grail said, taking note that Elvis now called him friend.

Robert leaned over and shook Grail's hand. "You wrote that book on the CSA, right? I read it."

"That's him," Elvis said. "Grail you're becoming a celebrity, bud. Better get used to it."

"I believe I might," he said as he sipped his champagne and sank a little deeper into the recliner. "I could get used to all this. Did you care for the book, Robert?"

"It was interesting."

"Very diplomatic," Grail said.

"So what's your claim to fame, Robert?" Elvis poured him a glass of champagne.

"Thanks. I'm a retired porn star, E."

Elvis and Grail quickly glanced at each other.

"Great champagne," Robert said. "I hear it cost a fortune."

Elvis fiddled with his baton, glanced again at Grail and then at Robert. "Porn star?"

"Yes, that's right. But retired. I gave it up a few years ago."

Grail sat up. "As in porn movies? That kind of porn star?"

"There isn't any other kind," Robert said. "You guys sure are quick."

"I'll be damned," Elvis said.

"What does a retired porn star do?" Grail said.

"Remembers fondly," Elvis said, slapping his knee and chuckling.

Robert smiled, held up a hand. "I know, I know. I've heard all the jokes. What can I say? Anybody with a couple bucks and a video store card can see me and my dick in all our glory."

"What was your porn name, Robert?" Grail was trying hard not to smirk.

"Wad Upshot," he said. "How's that for pizzazz?"

"That's a good one," Elvis said. "You know, I met some porn guy in Vegas last year, at a convention. A porky guy with wiry hair. He looked like an Arab."

"Ron Jeremy?" Robert said.

"Yeah, man. That's the guy. A friend of yours?"

"No. Like I said, I left that stuff behind."

"So, what *do* you do?" Grail said. "What's next after screwing for a living?" He immediately felt dumb. "Sorry, Robert. I didn't mean for it to come out quite so—"

"Graphically? It's OK. I've learned it's part of the permanent territory of who I am—was."

"I hear you, son," Elvis said. "I made some big mistakes in my life, but I'm still here. There were times in the old days when my L.A. house was like a porn movie, so I know what you mean. A man can change. But what can I do for you? Wade said it was important you met me. Why?"

The million dollar question, Robert thought, and for a moment he was afraid he would panic and not be able to make sense of it and would just appear to be a fool, some pathetic fringe celebrity drifting from fringe to fringe until there were no more fringes and he was lost for good. But in Elvis he heard sympathy. He knew what Elvis had overcome. The man had earned the best prize of all, the one Robert craved but until now didn't quite know how to get: redemption. You had to *do* something to get redemption. It wasn't automatic. It was conferred after a victory. Elvis had won his victory by not dying, by finding his way back to reality. Robert stared at the bloated but victorious Elvis. Still alive. Still king. The man still had an aura, and from it Robert felt—fueled. Robert felt something coming, felt a linkage engaged, some rusty gears breaking loose. His mind began to sense redemption by association. Yes, that was it. He began to smile a smile like no other that had ever ripped across his face. The idea had come. He had the angle. He *knew*. The journey from California was meant to culminate at this spot, with this idea.

"Robert?" Elvis switched his baton from and to hand.

Robert got up and paced the length of the room once, felt Elvis's and Grail's eyes follow him. He whirled and faced them, confident. The last fragments of the guilt that was Wad Upshot faded, flickered, became dead embers, and were gone for good.

"I wasn't just a porn star," he said. "I operated cameras. I learned lighting. I learned to judge a potential set like…the way maybe Robert E. Lee learned to assess terrain for battle." He paused, caught his breath, but felt strong, in control. He *knew*.

Elvis was grinning. "This is going to be good, Grail. I can feel it. I feel a pitch coming."

"Sure sounds like it." Grail looked around for the champagne bottle.

"Yes—a pitch, E." Robert took a breath, held it, and exhaled slowly, felt comfortable, felt like he was hovering above himself and watching from a corner of the ceiling. "I can make a movie, E. I know how to make a fucking movie. Production. Sound. Cameras. The whole shebang. I can produce it. I can direct it. I even have some money to get it off the fucking ground."

Elvis was on the edge of his seat. Grail had set his glass down.

"So make a movie," Elvis said. "By God do it."

"Yeah, but I want to make *your* movie, Elvis."

Elvis jumped up and slashed at air with quick karate chops. "I knew it. I knew it had to be something like that. The old magic never dies, I suppose."

"What are we talking here," Grail said. "Elvis does Dallas?"

Elvis thrust a chop toward Grail but pulled it. "You're getting a sense of humor, Grail. But I'm too old to drop my pants with a beach full of naked girls. That's not what Robert has in mind—is it, Robert?" To Grail Elvis sounded faintly hopeful.

"Not at all. Leave porn to the morons and narcissists in California. What I'm talking about is a documentary. The story of how you went to the brink but made it back. I would follow you with a camera. You would tell your own story, in your own words."

"And you would become a legit filmmaker," Grail said. "Elvis's redemption would also be yours."

"Yes. Absolutely." Robert had a flash of fear, worried the ghost of Wad Upshot might yet roar into the room and spoil the deal. "But it's a good story. And I can tell it. I can film it. When it's done, and when it's good—it will be good, I promise you—then all people will remember is the story, not who filmed it."

He held out his hand toward Elvis, who eyed it for so long Grail began to feel embarrassed for Robert, who nonetheless refused to take the hand back. He just kept it outstretched and looked hard into Elvis's eyes. Elvis fingered his sunglasses some more. Robert began to waver, to sweat, his arm trembled, and he was holding his breath. Suddenly Elvis shot his arm out and grasped Robert's hand.

"Ok, mister Wad the retired porno star. Let's make a movie. But it's not a deal unless you agree to one condition."

Robert let his breath out. "Yes—anything."

"I'll let you follow me around with a camera," Elvis said. "I'll answer any question. I'll talk about any issue—the drugs, the girls. Any of it. But the movie takes place on the road, starting tomorrow."

"On the road where?" Grail said. "You're not suggesting what I think you are—are you?"

"Yeah, man, I am. The road to find your dad. The three of us."

"Shit," Grail said. "You're really crazy, E. You know that? Really crazy."

"I know it," Elvis said. "But don't you want to find out who he is, man? Don't you want to know? You may never get another chance."

Grail chewed his lip a moment, knew finally that Elvis was right. It was an astounding feeling that descended on Grail, this concern from Elvis Presley for his welfare. He knew Elvis wanted to get something from it, too—the satisfaction of helping someone reach out to a father, something no longer possible for him. But still it was pretty noble of Elvis to even push for it. Grail knew it was a sign of how far Elvis had come back from the depths of madness toward something resembling the ability to live daily like real people did. And Grail knew, too, perhaps more honestly than ever before, that he did want to solve the mystery and confront the man, his father—or whatever he was. "Ok. Why not? Shit. Why the fuck not? We'll need a car, you know."

"I'll have a Cadillac delivered tomorrow," Elvis said.

"You and those damn Cadillacs," Grail said. "Ok, then we're doing it." Grail now understood it was something beyond his ability to control. A tide rising outside of him and sweeping him away but with benevolence—with love? He and Elvis were now like brothers. How unexpected and unlikely, but nonetheless it had come to pass and Grail wondered: was it really love? Love was elusive and muddy as a stream that had been tracked through too many times leaving it wet but cloudy, altered. This odyssey about to launch was many things. It was mystery and curiosity, and apparently it was also love. Love for Elvis? He guessed that was so. He guessed the benevolence of others was making it easier for him to really love, to apply the newfound power of love to other situations. To Darla, for example. That required more thought, but he sensed a door had creaked open and could be pushed further. It was dizzying but thrilling, and he forced himself back into the moment with the knowledge that all that had just raced through his mind—love, benevolence, opportunity—all of it just *was*. It existed without the need to be analyzed any more.

Grail realized Robert had been speaking to him, the words sounding far away.

"Your dad is missing?" Robert said.

"It's a long story," Grail said with a smile. "But I'm beginning to think it's a good one. I'll tell you on the road."

"Yeah, baby," Elvis said. "It's a road trip. It'll be fun."

And Grail sensed more, that Elvis was being pulled as much by the need to be the young Elvis, to once again touch, however briefly and tenuously, the freedom that young Elvis once had and had taken for granted until it had been plucked from him and he became marked for a death he had narrowly escaped.

"You need this road trip, don't you, E,"

"More than you know, Grail."

There was a knock at the door and a secret service agent peeked in and announced it was time to escort Elvis to the dais to sing.

Elvis tossed his baton to Grail. "Watch that thing for me, will you? It just gets in the damn way."

"Should we wait here for you, E?" Robert said. "Hell no," Grail said. "He's going to sing Love Me Tender while America gets put back on the map. If I were you I'd try and find a camera and get that movie started."

Chapter 21

▼

It was the mother of all Cadillacs, a red El Dorado convertible with a white leather interior and green and yellow dice hanging from the rear view mirror. Elvis had driven it around to the front of the Radisson himself, resplendent in his trademark shades, a cowboy hat, gold denim shirt, white linen pants, cowboys boots emblazoned with stars, and gold "E" cufflinks. It was his notion of incognito. It was old Elvis trying to be young Elvis; but he was clearly pleased with himself and showed no signs of relinquishing the wheel.

Grail, in a blue oxford shirt, khakis, and loafers exited the hotel's revolving door and was halted in his tracks by the glistening sight of the Caddy. He looked it over, from the high tail fins to the massive hood and shiny leather interior. Stepping to his right to see a bumper sticker on the brilliant chrome front bumper, he saw it read Viva Las Vegas.

"This is for you," Elvis said, and handed him a cowboy hat like his. Grail reluctantly tried it on, but discovered to his surprise he liked it. The hat bestowed a sense of freedom to be whoever he liked, an essential quality, he realized, for sudden odysseys into uncharted territory.

Grail climbed in, admired the glittering dashboard and instrument panel. "Yeah, E, we'll sure be inconspicuous as we roll through those quiet Maryland hamlets in this thing. Does it have machine guns behind the front grille?"

"It's a Caddy, man. Would you prefer a Volkswagen pissant, like you drive?"

"Passat."

"Right, Passat," Elvis said. "A forest green Passat. This is a cherry red Caddy. Will it do?"

"It'll more than do, E. It's perfect for a traveling medicine show like ours. Let's go get Robert and hit the road."

"Are you psyched, Grail?"

"I'm psyched." Grail thought it might even be true.

"Amen, brother," Elvis said. "But before we go one inch, maybe I ought to ask a pretty important question."

"Yeah?"

"Where the hell do we start looking to find your old man?"

"We never really talked about that, did we," Grail said. "A fine bunch of explorers that makes us." It made Grail suddenly question the wisdom of the trip, but he shook it off quickly. He was committed. He just wasn't sure what he was committed to.

"I figured it would come out in time," Elvis said. "But now is the time. The train done left the station."

"Maryland, my friend." Grail pointed in what he figured to be east. "That way, more or less."

"That's north." Elvis threw the Caddy into gear and eased onto Virginia Avenue. "What part of Maryland, bubba? I mean, you do have a general idea, right? Some *part* of Maryland?"

Grail thought about it. There was something his mother had said. Back in Kalamazoo, when she had told him his father was alive. What was it? An offhand remark about some place. It was there, on the dark edge of memory, and he could almost grasp it, could almost make it tumble down and cascade out his mouth, but not quite. It would come, though. It had to.

"I mean," Elvis continued, "it's not that big a state, I admit, but on a map you realize it stretches here and yonder from the Atlantic to the bay and then dribbles itself north and west along Pennsylvania. I got all the time in the world, but we do need some sort of plan."

"I know," Grail said. "I'm working on it. There is a place. My mother mentioned it. Don't worry, It'll come to me."

They drove through Georgetown, Elvis making a wrong turn once and getting lost for a few minutes but managing to find his way back to Chancellorsville Avenue for the leg up to Bethesda. As they left the district for Bethesda, Grail abruptly looked back and studied the cars behind them.

"It just occurred to me," he said. We're being followed, right? What about those State agents that keep track of us." He looked at one car, a brown sedan, and imagined it was the type they would drive. There were two men in it. He kept tabs on it for several miles.

Elvis pulled to the curb a couple blocks down from the Bethesda Holiday Inn, Robert's hotel. Grail noticed that the brown sedan kept going and the men didn't even glance their way. "Why are we stopping? That's Robert's hotel up there."

"I've been meaning to tell you something," Elvis said. "I saw that Mallory character this morning."

"He's an odd bird," Grail said. "I don't know if I would trust that guy about much."

"I hear you," Elvis said. "The security boys laugh about him behind his back, say he's a prima donna. But he's connected and knows things, if you get my drift."

"Is this about my father?"

"It is. It hasn't hit the news yet, but Wade said they arrested the guys who set off that bomb last week. They got them last night in Virginia."

"My father?" Grail felt anxious. It surprised him.

"Your pa wasn't with them. Wade says they don't think there's really a connection. Your pa just knew them, that's all."

"He's not a terrorist? Is that what Wade said?"

"That's right. Now he's just your pa."

"That's something to think about," Grail said.

"Yeah it is," Elvis agreed.

"But you'd think Wade would have come to me with the news," Grail said. "I don't understand that."

"He was on his way when I saw him. I told him to let me tell you."

"Thanks. There isn't anything more, is there? I mean, you're not holding out anything, are you, E?"

"No sir. That's all there is. Except we're on our own. No more security."

"Better that way," Grail said. "They'd just get in the way."

Elvis gunned the Caddy back into traffic and up to the Holiday Inn. A smiling Robert was waiting outside clutching a video camera.

"Some car," Robert said. He climbed in the back, the camera already rolling. "Does it have machine guns under the hood?"

"We already had that discussion," Elvis said. "How are you today, Robert?"

"I'm good. I feel real good. Ready to roll on this film, and ready to roll on Grail's mission."

"My God," Grail said. "It even has a name." But he wasn't unhappy about it. Instead he was relaxing and more willing to let it just happen. There would be plenty of time to try and make sense of it later.

Elvis gave him a friendly nudge with his elbow. "Grail's mission. Has a good ring to it."

"Roger that, E. It's like we're flying a B-17. You're the pilot and I'm the navigator, except the navigator is still trying to read the map and figure out where we should go."

"Relax," Elvis said. "Let it just come."

Robert put the camera down. "We don't know where we're going? It would help if I knew so I can think about how I'll set up shots."

"You're just going to film as we go, right?" Elvis said. "No script, just on the fly?"

"Absolutely," Robert said. "I plan to shoot the whole damn trip, or as much as I can, and let the footage speak for itself."

"Then just keep shooting. Grail will eventually tell us where we're going."

They rambled through Rockville and Gaithersburg, and then Elvis spotted a Tastee Freeze and wheeled the Caddy into the lot. "Strategy meeting," he said, and they all piled out to the counter and ordered chocolate cones. The girl behind the counter recognized Elvis and called the other girls to the front. Elvis signed autographs and then they adjourned to a picnic table under a maple tree.

"A chocolate ice cream cone gets pretty underestimated until you have one in your hand," Grail said. "Great idea, E."

"Amen," Elvis said.

"Listen," Robert said, "since we're sort of in the pre-planning stage here, can I make a suggestion?"

"You're the director," Grail said.

"Well, I remember hearing E sing Dixie, and the other one, uh, you know, the one with grapes of wrath and mine eyes have seen the glory."

"Battle Hymn of the Republic," Grail said.

"Yeah, that's the one.

"I haven't sung those two in a long time," Elvis said. "What made you think of them?"

"It came to me when I saw a sign back aways that said Harpers Ferry. Just north of there is Antietam. My ninth grade civics class went there. Why don't we go? Elvis singing those songs would be great. Elvis and an expert on the war visiting the battlefield."

"The bloodiest field of the war," Grail said. "I have to admit, in the wake of reunification, E, it could be some scene."

"Amen," Elvis said. "Mount up, men."

Grail didn't think Antietam—or Sharpsburg to the CSA—was where he'd find his father, but when they cruised through the quaint valley sheltering Harpers Ferry, the sun brilliant and warm on the Potomac River, Grail remembered something from James Joyce, something about the long way around being the shortest way home.

Chapter 22

▼

Grail was propped against a door in the back seat of the Caddy, his feet up on the back of the seat. He could see Robert filming Elvis as they roamed Antietam's famous Bloody Lane, the sunken road that was a death trap for so many Confederate soldiers in 1862. Beyond the lane he could see the statue of Robert E. Lee, his old friend, looming over the green fields. Leaning against its granite base was a flock of park rangers tickled to see Elvis up close and personal. Elvis waved to Grail, then looked into Robert's camera and began singing, bits and snatches of the words drifting up the gentle rise. It was Dixie and then the Battle Hymn of the Republic, as promised, and what Grail could catch of them sounded lovely. The man could sing.

After a while he lost interest in Elvis and Robert and heard the mournful calls of doves in the oak tree above the Caddy. He could see them, a gray pair with bobbing heads. There were plump robins and nervous sparrows, too, and tiny yellow finches flitting from limb to limb; but it was the sad doves that set the tone, that reminded Grail these fields and rolling hills had been America's greatest killing ground.

Still, Grail was not unhappy or sad. Antietam did not repel him, and soon the doves disappeared, leaving Grail a little sleepy, the creeping but warm approach of true sleep and not the exhaustive need to escape a thunderous reality. He kicked off his loafers and stripped away his socks. A small breeze washed through the cracks in his toes, tickling his ankles. The afternoon sun was bashful, preferring to slip in and out of a band of ivory clouds. Through a break in the branches above him a silent jet slowly crawled across the sky.

His eyes fluttered and his breathing slowed. Grail let his eyes close. The sparrows chattered as though next to his ears. The branches of the tree swayed in the breeze and to Grail it sounded like the rustlings of a sweeping broom. A far off voice from a tourist abruptly sounded close, an acoustical anomaly, he suspected, and it made him think of the star-crossed George Pickett who feasted on shad with other officers while a similar anomaly masked the sound of his division in combat just a short distance away. He could envision the dashing Pickett in the impeccable gray uniform of a CSA major-general, the oiled ringlets of hair brushing his shoulders; but when sleep did come it was Lee, not Pickett, who came to Grail.

Lee's white hair was longer, his white moustache droopy and chaotic. Grail was struck by how much he resembled Albert Einstein. Instead of the kimonos or dress uniform Lee wore a simple dark blazer, tie, and white shirt, further amplifying the Einstein resemblance. As always, Lee appeared to sit on an invisible chair or bench.

"How are you, son?" Lee said.

"Fine. I'm OK. How's life in the great beyond?"

"Always hectic," Lee said. "I've joined a group that plays cards every Friday and Monday."

"What happened to checkers?"

"I needed some variety."

"Do you like cards?"

"Not so much. But Gen. Pope and Mr. Fighting Joe Hooker play, too, and I enjoy beating them, just like when I was down there."

"Is it really *down* here and *up* there?"

"No, it's more like simultaneous dimensions, but saying down and up is less intimidating, perhaps. But you don't—"

"I know, I know," Grail said. "I don't have the clearance for that information."

"Why worry about it until it's time?" Lee said. "God's will. Besides, you have so many more pressing issues, right?"

"Yeah, I suppose I do. Say, general, do you know you resemble Albert Einstein for some reason? He lived after you did. He was a great scientist."

Lee grinned broadly. "I can tell you he's some fellow that Mr. Einstein. He really tickles me. He does. Smart as a whip. He makes us laugh at the card games."

"He's a regular at your group?"

"He shows up from time to time. Sometimes I see him lost in thought off by himself. I try not to bother him when he's thinking. He thinks so hard and so well. Longstreet brought him to the game the first time. I liked Mr. Einstein right off."

Grail became pensive and Lee noticed. "Just spit it out, son. Whatever it is, don't bottle it up."

"Right," Grail said, reminding himself it was a dream, but of course he had also learned that dreams seemed to be more and so he no longer underestimated them. "Do you know where I'm at, general? My body, I mean."

"Yes, you're at Sharpsburg—Antietam to the federals."

"You actually know that?" Grail said. "From up there?"

"Surely, son. It's no big trick."

"That's amazing. I guess it means there's truly a link between the living and the dead."

"You can't quote me on that one, son." Lee said "But please, go on."

"Well, I'm here, at Antietam, with this guy named Elvis and another guy named Robert, who used to be called Wad Upshot. He used to be porno star. You know about porno?"

"Sure I do. We have some of those folks up here, too."

"Really? They made it? Well, you probably don't have anyone like Elvis up there."

"But we know about him," Lee said. "It was almost his time when he was still fairly young—42, I believe. It was close. But it was judged to be an error. It was too soon. Some day he'll make a pretty eclectic addition for us."

"I hear you," Grail said. "Don't be fooled by that simpleton act he sometimes pulls. He knows more than he lets on."

"Thanks for the advice, son. I'll bear it in mind."

So, general, how do you feel about me being at Antietam? I mean, does it bring back memories?"

"Oh, I'm well past the memories, son. Everyone that was there is here, and we're all reconciled to our places in history. But how about *you*? How do *you* feel about being there? Have you strayed from your path?"

"I'm trying to decide that," Grail said. "Robert wanted to film Elvis here. He's making a documentary on Elvis."

"And you?"

"Well," Grail said, "it's a chance to relax and try and figure some things out."

"And what have you figured out?"

"Where to look for my father, I guess."

"Where *is* your father?"
You could tell me, right?" Grail said.
"I could. But it's better if I don't."
"Right," Grail said. "I figured as much. Well, that's OK, because I think he's to be found in my head. A man's father ultimately is in his head. It's what you want to make of it."
"I see," Lee said. "Now I feel like the one who doesn't have clearance for information.
What do you mean?"
"I mean that a father can be good or bad or missing or whatever, but the son has to find a way to live regardless. If the father is good, then the son's job is much easier. Maybe then it's a problem of living in a large shadow. But if the father is bad, then the son must really become his own father. He must raise himself and learn good from bad somehow. If he makes it then he can pity the bad father, but ultimately the son has to be his own father."
"Interesting. Have you then assumed your father is evil?"
"Maybe not evil," Grail said. "But not good. My mother left him when she learned he was a southern radical, a racist. He may even have been in the KKK. I don't for sure on that. I hope to find out. For a while I thought he might be a terrorist. Maybe his sin in that area is that he pals around with terrorists. I don't know that, yet.
"Then isn't it too soon to follow your theory so rigidly?" Lee said. "This notion of being your own father out of necessity. Too soon for that?"
"Maybe. I sense I'll know very soon."
"Are you in much pain over it?" Lee said.
"When I was younger, sure. But I survived it. I made it. I became a man. I'm a good man. I know it from how I treat people and the decisions I make. I consider others. I know the difference between making a living and greed. I possess tolerance and compassion and curiosity. I can be wrong and admit it. I still make mistakes, sometimes make poor judgments, but I know it when it happens and I don't try and deny it. For God's sake I love cats."
"And still there are dark days." Lee said.
"Yes. But I get through them somehow. I get past them without becoming bad, and that makes all the difference."
"There is one quality you didn't mention," Lee said. "Do you possess patience?"
Grail thought a moment. "I believe I do, yes."

"I hope so. I fear it is the one you will need to rely on most. That and compassion."

"You mean when I meet up with my father, right?"

"Yes, that's what I mean. More than that I can't say. You must make of it what you will. But then, your theory says as much. Good luck, Grail."

"This is the last time, isn't it," Grail said. "We won't meet again."

"You don't need me anymore," Lee said.

Grail studied Lee, who no longer much resembled Einstein. Now he was just Lee. The Lee of history.

Lee saluted and then dissolved. There was no hurtling along dark caverns this time for Grail, just warm and wet blackness, slowly giving way to light.

Chapter 23

From green and shallow Bloody Lane Robert panned his camera up the rise until it framed Grail, who was leaning against the trunk of the Caddy. The sun emerged from cloud momentarily and the chrome bumpers gleamed. Grail threw a snappy salute at the camera and smiled.

As he filmed, Robert said, "Dr. Grail Hudson, CSA expert and professor of history at the University of Illinois, surveys the sunken road that became notorious as Bloody Lane, the scene of so much carnage in 1862. Here Gen. Anderson's North Carolinians fought and died in bloody heaps."

Elvis tapped Robert on the shoulder. "He's smiling, Bob. Is that cool for what happened here? We don't want this to turn goofy like one of my old beach movies."

"Good point, E." Robert yelled for Grail to cut the smile and then he shot Grail's intro again. This time Grail looked determined.

"Better," Elvis said. "Where do you want me now?"

"Let's do a q and a session on how you got to know Grail. We'll do it in jumps, from one spot to another and eventually walk our way up to the car, where we can formally introduce Grail."

"You're the director," Elvis said. "Where to?"

"The statue."

Elvis sat on the base of the Lee statue, his ample belly seeping over his belt, and looked hopefully into the camera.

"Let's do it standing," Robert said. "More flattering. Try a reflective pose."

"Gotcha." Elvis crossed his arms over his chest and leaned against the granite base.

"How's this?"

"Beautiful. Now we're rolling, E. Tell us how you met Dr. Hudson."

"I met Grail in Washington, just before the reunification gig. I had read his book, and then was lucky to have coffee with him at Starbucks, which by the way makes the best coffee."

"Good, E. But I don't think we need to do a plug for Starbucks. This is a documentary."

"Right, man. Let's do it again."

After several takes Elvis had it down and Robert followed him as he strolled silently through the lane. Earlier he had sang "Battle Hymn of the Republic" and "Dixie," had done them slow and with obvious feeling and affection, and it had moved Robert almost to tears.

Robert followed Elvis out of the lane to a split rail fence. Elvis climbed up and sat astride it, happily, like he was a kid again. Robert filmed him from the waist up to hide the paunch.

"You and Dr. Hudson have become good friends," Robert said, pointing a finger to the camera to induce Elvis to look right into it.

"Yeah, man, that's right. I don't know, it's like we're family, sort of."

"How so?"

"Well, Grail has never met his pa, and my pa has been dead a long time. We're in the same boat, just for different reasons. That's why we're on the road now, to help Grail find his pa."

"And will you find something in the process, Elvis?"

Elvis looked away, at Bloody Lane, and then back into the camera. "Satisfaction, I guess. The satisfaction of helping a man who still has a chance to see his pa."

"That's where it gets a little complicated," Robert said. "Isn't there some controversy surrounding Grail's father, who is reported to be living somewhere in Maryland, and whose background was investigated by the CSA state department?"

"They thought Grail's pa might be linked to those radicals," Elvis said. "The ones that set off a bomb. But they looked into it and found he just knew the wrong folks, is all. It was people he grew up with. He wasn't personally involved."

"What's the next step on this odyssey to locate Grails' father?"

"Well, we'll know that pretty soon, I reckon. Grail has some ideas about where to look and I suspect we'll know it pretty soon."

"You've undertaken this journey on just the faith that Grail will know where to go, Elvis. And then that his father can even be found. Why?"

"Faith is the best reason of all. My gut just tells me Grail's a good man. We all need faith in something or someone. My faith is in Grail. I want to give him the chance to find his pa. What he does with it is out of my hands and up to him. I was given a second chance. Now I'm helping him have his."

Grail came down the gentle rise and joined them.

"Would you turn off the camera, Robert?" Grail said. "I want to talk to you two."

"I still need to do a formal intro of you, Grail. You know, a sort of tight shot where you express some thoughts on Antietam. I already identified you in the long shot."

"Later," Grail said. "There'll be time for that later." Robert and Elvis both sensed a new tone in Grail's voice. He sounded confident, focused.

"What's up, Grail?" Elvis said.

Grail walked down to the split rail fence, Elvis and Robert in tow. Grail placed his hands on the fence, looked down into the lane.

"The poor bastards that filled this sorry excuse for cover, what did they die for? What does any soldier die for? That's the eternal question."

Robert's camera was rolling, and Grail noticed. "That's OK, Robert. Fire away."

Elvis joined Grail, was surveying the lane, trying to see what he only felt Grail could see. "They were brave old boys," Elvis said. "Both sides."

"Yes," Grail said. "The North Carolinans were brave here, and the Federal Irish Brigade was brave, too, out there." Grail pointed toward a field. "No damn cover at all out there."

Robert sat his camera down, the enormity of the history finally getting to him, too. He leaned against the fence, next to Grail. "What *did* they die for? What *do* soldiers die for?"

A strong breeze came up, a nearby maple tree's limbs creaking and groaning, sounding all too human, and all three men had the same thought.

"Ghosts?" Elvis said.

"Why not?" Robert said. "Prove to me there aren't ghosts. There's a lot of things that can't be explained."

Grail nodded. "And if there are ghosts, there's more here than just about anywhere."

"What makes a man be in a fix like they had here?" Robert said. "Why do soldiers do it?"

"They're all looking for something," Grail said. "A lot of them, anyway. The inexhaustible journey for the truth. Or a truth. Any truth. They believe the truth is wrapped in a cause. But I imagine that many don't know why they do it. They just do. One day they're safe on their farm, or in some town, and then suddenly they're kneeling in Bloody Lane, or advancing across an open field with a lot of other men, no different than them, and they're looking into the guns and then it's too late for philosophy and causes and slogans. Then it just is, and what happens next gets trusted to God. Listen to us, talking like they were still alive."

Robert chuckled. "I'm sorry. I'm not laughing at you. But that's how I got into porn. I just realized it." He chuckled some more.

"How do you figure?" Elvis said.

"This will be good," Grail said. "The Wad Upshot story."

"Good old Wad," Robert said. Well, it's like Grail says. One day I was running the 220 and 440 in high school in Alexandria, just taking life one day at a time, not paying attention to much beyond what it took for me to be happy, to have fun, the days blending together, and then another day comes and I'm in California making porn with a whole bunch of boys and girls who can't pinpoint the event or reason that led them to that place."

"We walk around sort of blind much of the time," Grail said. "Changes come and we don't see them. We just wake up to them. We don't watch for signs, or recognize hints. We're not careful. Then we look around and wonder how we got to a place. And then time is up."

"That brings up regrets," Robert said.

"What if," Elvis agreed.

"Regrets," Grail said. "Well, I'm through with them."

"I told you," Elvis said to Robert. "Here it comes. Where to?"

"Ok," Grail said. "Here's the deal. When I woke up a while ago something came into focus, something my mom said about my father. I've been trying to remember it for acouple days."

"You know the town he's in?" Elvis said.

"Maybe," Grail said. "The CSA boys surely looked for him in his hometown, across the bay from Annapolis. A little burg called Tunis Mills. But my mom said when he was a kid he ran away from home sometimes and camped a lot down the bay on a coupleislands—Bloodsworth Island and Marsh Island. It's a guess, but an educated one. I think he might be there."

"It's as good a guess as any," Elvis said. "Makes sense to me."

"I'm just the camera man," Robert said. "Let's go."

"Now you're the director, Grail," Elvis said.

"Yeah, I guess so."

They fired up the Caddy and drove into Frederick and caught I-70 east. In Baltimore Elvis wanted to stop for some crabs. As they started south to Annapolis Robert leaned over the front seat and said, "From Bloody Lane to Bloodsworth Island. You know, that's not a bad title for the film."

Chapter 24

It was Elvis who suggested they camp out. They had lingered a bit in Annapolis to watch a Confederate Navy frigate slipping down the Severn River, and then they crossed the Chesapeake Bay Bridge and went south to Cambridge, but it was getting close to sunset, so Elvis stopped at a TruValue store and bought a huge tent, a cooler, a Coleman stove, cots, sleeping bags, deck chairs, and whatever else struck his notion of roughing it. The store owner threw in a free axe and fuel for the stove after Elvis sang a few seconds of "Hound Dog." Next door at the Rebel Cause Mini-Mart they stocked up on Coors beer, hot dogs, buns, potato salad, and chocolate cake. On Highway 50 a mile south of Cambridge they spotted a creek meandering through a thick stand of trees and that was where they pitched the tent.

"You planning on taking all this stuff with us tomorrow, E?" Grail said while he and Elvis pounded tent stakes into the ground. Robert went off to chop wood.

"Naw. Too much dang trouble. We'll leave it for the next campers who come along."

"Good idea," Grail said. "Somebody can throw up a sign that says Elvis slept here and it'll be a moneymaker."

"Wouldn't surprise me none," Elvis said. "I reckon once we get down to Bloodsworth there'll be a motel, but this idea just struck me. I haven't camped out since I don't know when."

"I was a boy scout in Michigan," Grail said. "Up by Houghton Lake. That was the last time for me."

"I guess for me it was when I was in the CSA Army, in Germany," Elvis said. "That's where I first got into trouble with drugs. Never again, brother. Never again. I like a few beers here and there and that's it."

They pulled a couple ice cold Coors out of the cooler and sat in the new deck chairs. Robert came back with an armload of wood and made a fire. Elvis stripped bark off some twigs with a pocketknife and made roasting sticks. The fire glowed orange and blue. The juice from the hot dogs dropped into the flames and hissed. It was dark except for the fire and the occasional pair of headlights dancing through the curve out on the road. They ate their hot dogs and potato salad and sipped the beers and felt good. Elvis produced a radio, another gift from the TrueValue owner, but he set the volume low, and the music, mostly rock and roll out of a Baltimore station, did not intrude.

"I like this one guy pretty well, Tom Petty," Elvis said as he bobbed his head with the beat. "I won't back down. You can stand me up at the gates of hell but I won't back down. Man, I like those lyrics. I think they'll just be my motto from here out."

"Me, too, E," Grail said. "Me, too."

When the Rolling Stones' "Satisfaction" came on Elvis slapped his knee. "You know, people always thought I didn't like the Stones. I guess that was a public persona thing, but the truth is I listened to them plenty at home. That was some badass group. Just a bunch of guys who loved the blues, like me."

"You ever meet them?" Grail said.

"A few years back Keith Richards came by my house in LA. We drank some beers and played guitar. I swear I couldn't understand a word that boy said, but he sure can play guitar."

"What about the Beatles, E?" Robert said.

"Man, they had something. Rare."

Grail said, "Didn't they come and play at your house back in the 60s? I always heard about some historical meeting."

"They did. That was some funny night. They came in and just stood around staring at me. I was getting nervous, like maybe they really didn't like me. I told them I'd just up and leave if somebody didn't say or do something, so John Lennon grabbed a guitar and off we went. I played some bass. We had us some fun that night. Played their stuff and then mine."

"And ever since," Robert said, "people have wished there was a record of it. Imagine what a recording of that session could bring. Why didn't somebody think to do it, E?"

"We did. I've still got it."

"No shit?" Robert said. "I've got to get this on film, E."

"No. Please. It's not a very good recording. Poor quality. It's just for me. I listen to it every now and then to remind myself of the old days."

"Why haven't the Beatles ever mentioned the recording, E?" Grail said.

"They don't know about it."

"Really?" Grail studied Elvis's face, thought he detected some regret or even embarrassment.

Elvis stoked the fire and impaled another hot dog on his stick. "One of my guys had a recorder in the room. I don't know why we didn't mention it. Maybe I had some reason back then, but so much has happened, so many years have gone by, that now it's just one of those decisions you make and later you don't understand it. But we never released it, so I didn't tell them, not even after John got shot. So it stays private. Maybe I'll call Paul McCartney one of these days and tell him about it. I don't know."

"We all have our secrets and mysteries," Grail said. "Don't sweat it, E. I don't think you did anything wrong."

"Thanks, man. Hey, that's enough of me, guys. Really. Let's talk about something else."

Name it, E," Grail said.

OK, bubba. Don't you have a lady somewhere back home in Illinois waiting for you?

Back there guarding your forest green Passat? You never mention it."

Grail squeezed mustard on his second hot dog and took a big bite. "Hard to beat a dog over an open flame," he said with his mouth full. "Great idea, E."

"Look who's avoiding the subject, Robert," Elvis said. He smacked Grail lightly on the arm with his stick.

"Pass me one of those dogs, E," Robert said. "I hear you. I think Grail has woman trouble."

"First he's got pa trouble," Elvis said, wiping beer off his chin. "And now woman trouble."

"Here's to Grail and all his troubles," Robert said. He and Elvis clinked beer cans together, beer sloshing on the ground."

"If you two are going to gang up on me at least pass me another beer," Grail said.

"And I don't have woman trouble. I have an opportunity. Maybe."

"Maybe?" Elvis said. "Who's the lucky lady anyway? Wait, you did mention a gal once back at the Radisson, right? Didn't you tell me about someone?"

"I don't think so, E. But her name is Darla. Darla Pinsky. She's a graduate student at Illinois."

"He dates his students," Robert said. "A cradle robber."

"No fucking way, Robert. Darla's 30, and she isn't one of my students. She's from Michigan, like me."

"Careful, Robert," Elvis said. "Or Grail might remind you about the porn biz."

"That's right, bubba," Grail said. He popped open another beer.

"Ouch," Robert said. "I guess I walked right into that one."

"You're forgiven," Grail said.

They ate hot dogs until they were stuffed, Elvis unable to stop farting for a while.

"They don't call me the king for nothing," he said. "But don't ask me to light any."

"Don't worry," Grail said. "What would your fans think if they could hear you now?"

"They'd think I ain't nothing but a hound dog."

They were still laughing when a car slowed out on the road and a spotlight was switched on. It was a Maryland state trooper. He pulled off the road and Elvis, who always had a soft spot for the police, met him down by the road. After a few minutes the trooper drove off.

"He just wanted to check on us," Elvis said when he came back and plopped down in his chair. "I guess it got all over town that we were planning to camp out."

"The perks of fame," Grail said. "Does it ever get to you?"

"Sometimes. But he gave us a good tip. He said if we can pull out pretty early we ought to. Seems there's talk about the townsfolk popping in to throw us a party in the morning. The mayor wants to hand out the key to the city and all that shit."

"Good God," Robert said. "I'm going to put it to bed. See you boys in the morning."

Robert went in the tent and Elvis and Grail could hear him unzip his sleeping bag. They sat quietly by the fire a while. Grail thought about what to say if he found his father, but nothing substantial would come. He tried very hard but had drunk a little too much and his mind wandered. He thought about his father but mostly he wondered about Darla. She had told him to make an adventure out of his trip. Well, he sure as hell had accomplished that.

Elvis produced a cell phone and handed it to Grail. "Hell, son, might as well give the little lady a ring."

Grail was tempted, then declined. He stared at the soft green light of the phone, wanting to dial the number but unsure if he should.

"Just do it," Elvis said. "Just say you were thinking of her. Ladies eat that up."

"We sort of had an arrangement when I left. She said I should do whatever I needed to do about my father. Not to worry about her or think about her until it was decided."

"Elvis chuckled. "Hell, son, that may be what she said, but it ain't what she meant, bubba. When a woman says don't think about me, or don't worry about me, she means exactly the opposite."

"You think so?"

"I know so, son. Ain't I Elvis Fucking Presley?"

"That's true, E. You are Elvis Fucking Presley."

"Dial the number."

Grail hesitated, finally said, "Ok. I'll call her. But you have to promise to say hello to her."

"Sure."

"Hey, what time is it, E? We're an hour ahead of Illinois, right?"

"Yeah, I think so." He looked at his watch. "It's a little after ten. Must be nine back there."

Darla answered on the third ring. Her voice startled Grail, who finally realized how long it had been.

"It's about time you called," Darla said. 'Did you fall off the earth?"

"I thought you said not to worry about calling?"

Elvis squeezed Grail's elbow. "Told you, bubba."

Darla said, "I know, but you were supposed to figure out that I really wanted you to call. It's been forever, Grail. Where are you?"

"Maryland. Uh, outside Cambridge, Maryland."

"Jesus," she said. "Where? Hold on while I grab my atlas."

"She's getting her atlas, E."

Elvis opened another beer.

"OK, I'm back," Darla said. "Yeah, I see it. Cambridge. Why are you in Cambridge?"

"I got a tip my father might be down here. We're going to a place called Bloodsworth Island, a little further south. I think he might be there. See it on your map?"

"Jesus," Darla said. "Yeah, I found it. What a name. You said we. Who's with you, Grail?"

"Elvis."

It was silent on Darla's end for a moment.

"I think we're at the part where she doesn't believe it, E," Grail said.

"Jesus," Darla finally said. "I saw you on the news a couple days ago at that reunification ball, standing next to Elvis. Is he really there, with you?"

"Right here. He's sitting here by the fire, drinking a Coors. In the flesh. We bought a tent and we're camping out by a creek outside Cambridge. Pretty cool, eh?"

Elvis raised his beer in salute.

"You're camping with Elvis Presley?" Darla said. "In the middle of nowhere? In Maryland?"

It suddenly sounded very cool to Grail. "Well, yeah."

"Ready?" Elvis said.

"I think so." He handed the phone to Elvis.

"Hey, baby," Elvis said. "Is this the famous Darla Pinsky, the pride of Michigan?"

She didn't say anything for a long moment, then, "is this really Elvis Presley?"

"You want me to sing something?"

"Well, shit, yeah," Darla said. "Like what?"

"Name it," Elvis said.

"Uh, Jesus. OK, that one about fools rushing in. Crap, I can't remember the title."

"I know the one," Elvis said, and he sang it. When he was done Darla chatted with Elvis like they were old friends.

"I'm going to bed," Grail told Elvis, but he knew he'd said all he needed to. He felt good. "Tell her I'll call her tomorrow." Elvis nodded.

A few minutes later he heard Elvis slipping into his sleeping bag in the cot opposite him. Robert snored from a corner of the tent.

"Any message for me, E?"

"Just that you'll be very welcome when you get home, bubba. Good night, Grail."

"Good night, Elvis." It sounded like he'd been saying it all his life.

Chapter 25

▼

Crossing the Nanticoke River Elvis spotted a roadside sign advertising a boat for sale. Blessed yet again with inspiration, he turned down a narrow lane to the river and traded the Caddy for a 40-foot cabin cruiser, the deal's lopsidedness countered by the fact the boat's owner figured an Elvis Caddy trumped the cruiser, which was, Grail discovered to his amusement, named The General Lee. Elvis got the owner to do a quick paint job, and the cruiser, now called Gladys and Vernon, lumbered southwest toward Bloodsworth Island with a proud Elvis at the helm.

Robert filmed wary herons and noisy flotillas of ducks along the shoreline, his mind already racing with angles for a documentary on the natural resources of Chesapeake Bay. Grail sagged pensively in one of the padded leather captains chairs next to Elvis and studied a map, occasionally scanning far downriver for something that he seemed to regard as just out of sight.

"It's not that far, E," Grail said. "When we get down in the Tangier Sound we'll be there."

"I know," Elvis said.

"I mean," Grail said, "that once we get in the sound we should see Bloodsworth Island, according to the map. Actually see it."

"And then we'll be there," Elvis said.

"Yes. Then we'll be there." Grail looked again far downriver, wondering how he would feel when the island came into sight, remembering that his father might not be there at all. He wondered how that would feel, too. Relief? Disappointment? Take your pick, he realized.

"Second thoughts?" Elvis said.

"Hell, E, my thoughts have already reached well into the hundreds."

"You'll be fine, man. Have you thought about what you'll say if he's down here?"

"I don't know," Grail said. "Maybe, good morning father—are you a terrorist?"

"An icebreaker," Elvis said.

"Exactly."

He grew quiet and knew Elvis was giving him room. Grail stared at the nearly unbroken forests of pine, cedar, and oak in battle line along the banks of the Nanticoke. The cruiser eased ahead smoothly, the water calm and green. There was no hurry. It was not far to the sound. But the thick solidarity of the trees made Grail think of something closing in. He was relieved later when the cruiser emerged from a bend and the river was wider. Just ahead, on the left bank, a cluster of houses crowded a wharf.

"We need food," Elvis said. "What do you think?"

"I could eat," Grail said.

Robert popped his head in the cabin with a pair of binoculars he had found below. "There's a little restaurant on that dock," he said. "I could see the sign."

"Hungry, Robert?" Elvis said.

"Famished."

They tied up alongside the wharf and went in the restaurant. It was small and spare, with a dozen wood tables whose surfaces had been nearly obliterated by people carving initials. A ceiling fan whirled fast overhead, causing the corners of napkins on the tables to curl up and wave. The place smelled faintly of antiseptic and was nearly empty save for a couple farmers drinking ice tea and a skinny teenage girl waiting tables. The cook was pale and plump and sat at the end of the lunch counter smoking a cigarette, his white cap and smock stained with grease. He smoked slowly, with obvious pleasure, and occasionally glanced at Elvis, certain he'd seen the face, but not sure where. After a while he shrugged and limped back to the kitchen.

The waitress was dull and seemed bored or tired, or both. She didn't recognize Elvis, either, and slowly brought them a round of Rolling Rock beer and platters of shrimp, crab, and cole slaw. Elvis had a cold glass of buttermilk after they ate.

"An old vice," he said. "One of the few I have left."

Robert fiddled with his camera but was not filming.

Grail had eaten silently, the others knowing what he must be thinking, and then he spread his map on the table and studied it.

"I think we can be there in a few hours," Grail said. "I'm not totally sure about distances, and our speed, but that seems reasonable—a few hours."

"We need supplies," Elvis said after a moment. "More food and stuff. That bait shop by the wharf had a sign that said it sells groceries."

"I'll go," Robert said. "You always buy too much, E."

Grail smiled. "You do, E. Time to travel a little lighter."

They met back at the wharf and loaded their provisions, all of them trying to gauge how long the expedition would last and what the final scene would be like. Grail had finally emerged as their leader, his opportunity for epiphany their true mission and destination.

"OK,' Grail said after they were under way. "This is how I see it. We'll be there very soon. We'll be in the sound, I mean, and we'll see the island. The map shows some places—some coves—where we can land, and that's it. We just pull up and drop anchor, or tie up to a tree, or whatever, and we step ashore. That's my plan. It'll never be accused of being too complicated. I don't know how long we'll be here. Maybe not long. I don't know."

"It sounds about right," Elvis said. "Don't need to be complicated."

"And then you'll go look for your father," Robert said. "If he's there."

"If he's there," Grail agreed.

"We've got plenty of grub and we can sleep on the boat," Elvis said. "We're set. Don't worry about time."

"Thanks, E," Grail said, thinking momentarily there should be more he should say to that, but quickly realizing thanks truly was enough, that Robert and Elvis didn't require more, were getting the more from being part of it. It was a love of sorts and Grail had known it for some time, could feel it. Three wounded men, not always conscious of their wounds, whose lives had somehow steered clear of basic and true love for a long time and for very different reasons, but who now knew they had been compelled to band together, to gather strength from their partnership, and to emerge on the other side of the odyssey in ways each was certain he would be able to feel but maybe never quite articulate. But the center, the heart, the soul of the partnership was Grail. Where the flamboyance of Elvis, his incredibly child-like innocence and curiosity had gotten them in a direction, now Grail had awakened and Elvis and Robert were now in the protection of his wake.

The cruiser increased speed, its bow wave tall and white. The Nanticoke banks had been widening for some time, the trees no longer oppressing Grail, who had stationed himself near the bow behind the desperate protection of a railing. A footnote of history bubbled up to his brain: Captain John Smith had discovered the Nanticoke a very long time ago, maybe 1600 and some change. Grail knew what that must have been like.

Chapter 26

▼

They were well into Tangier Sound, the water suddenly dotted with whitecaps rolling angrily into the cruiser's hull. Grail wiped spray from his face and tightened his grip on the railing. Ahead he could make out a tall shape, like a fat smokestack, and realized it must be the Bloodsworth Island lighthouse he'd seen on his map. He pointed ahead and looked over his shoulder to Elvis and Robert behind the cruiser's windshield, but they had already spotted the island and were giving him thumbs up.

Grail returned the thumbs up, but it seemed to take forever for the cruiser to survive the buffeting waves and inch closer to the island. It was as though a mysterious force was subtly working against them, trying to prevent—what? Grail felt like everything except his emotions had been reduced to slow motion. Too much time to think, to speculate. He didn't want theory anymore. He wanted action. Movement. Decision. Resolution? He didn't know what that was, how it applied here. But he longed for it.

The wet and battered cruiser finally slipped into the shelter of Piney Island Cove. Elvis eased it along the bank and Grail jumped ashore with the bow line and tied it to a tree trunk while Robert filmed him. A startled Great Blue Heron suddenly broke into flight, skimming just above the water across the cove toward the lighthouse. Chattering gulls circled overhead. Bands of ducks plied the shoreline or squatted in platoons in the tall grass. Grail led Elvis and Robert inland, where they quickly discovered that Bloodsworth Island was mostly a wetlands paradise for birds and waterfowl.

Robert had bought three pairs of roomy rubber boots on the advice of an old salt at the bait shop and they needed them. They squished and slipped their way along as they cut around the cove and headed toward the lighthouse. Grail figured that was as good a place to start as any, but it proved to be empty. The lighthouse was decaying, its bricks chipped and weathered badly.

"I don't think they use this light anymore," Grail said. He was disappointed that they didn't at least find evidence that someone had been here recently.

"Does anybody even live on this island?" Robert said. "I mean permanently. Is there a town?"

"I don't think so," Grail said. "There isn't one on the map."

"It's too dang marshy," Elvis said. "I guess only birds like it here."

"And Grail's dad," Robert said.

"Yeah," Grail said. "My dad. If he's even here. Maybe it's a wild goose chase we're on."

"This is the place for a goose alright," Elvis said. "This could be goose heaven."

Grail frowned. "That might be all we're going to find on this godforsaken island."

"Too soon to give up," Elvis said. "You haven't have you?"

Grail stared at the ground a moment, and then off in the distance. "I guess not. Not yet."

They decided to take a break and sat at the base of a tree in one of the few dry spots they had encountered.

"This island really isn't that big," Grail said after a while. "Why don't we split up? That Ok with you guys?"

"Yeah, man," Elvis said. "What do you have in mind?"

Grail thought it over a moment, recalled the map: "The south end has what looks like a beach, or something resembling one. Hard to tell, but it's worth a look. I'm going down there.

"Sounds right," Robert said. "What about us?"

"E, how about checking the west side," Grail said. "Robert, go to the north end. That ought to cover it. If he's here one of us ought to know it, or at least see some signs of life somewhere, an old campfire—something."

"OK," Elvis said.

"Let's meet back at the boat in about two hours," Grail said. "That's enough time, I think."

Grail headed south at a quick pace. When he reached Lower Island Point he walked West along the shore. He figured if anything he would at least work his way west and up that shore toward Elvis, who he feared might get lost. It wouldn't do to be known as the man who lost Elvis on a deserted island. He was glad he still had a sense of humor, could see the world beyond himself, though he was anxious to solve the mystery of his father, and now he worried it would remain a mystery.

He trudged along but saw no one, detected no tracks, found no cold campfires. He had walked far enough west to see several small islands off the southwest shore of Bloodsworth. He recalled that one of them was Adam Island, and that seemed oddly enough appropriate, for if his father was here he was sort of like Adam wandering in his own private Eden, but with no Eve in sight. That struck Grail as funny but he couldn't quite say why. And he reminded himself that Bloodsworth really wasn't much of an Eden. A dead end seemed more likely.

More than an hour had passed. Grail knew it would soon be time to make his way back to the others. He was well up the west coast of the island where he surely thought he would run into a grinning Elvis at any turn. At Bloodsworth Point he sat on a log for a minute to rest and enjoy the view of Chesapeake Bay. There had been no sign of Elvis, but Grail could envision him crashing though the brush and emerging suddenly, but happily, though looking as out of place in the wild as any man alive.

At first that's who he thought it was, the figure meandering along the shore well ahead of him, and he grinned, thinking, Elvis is just a 64-year-old teenager endlessly looking for adventure. But it wasn't Elvis, or Robert. It was a stranger, a man in a windbreaker and jeans and a baseball cap, and all of Grail's logic said it must be Lewis Hudson, his father, for who else could be on this damn island? The man mostly stared at the ground, or out at Chesapeake Bay, as he strolled, seemingly relaxed, apparently not lost or out of time and instead where he should be.

Grail walked toward him. They were several hundred yards apart and still the man had not noticed him. Grail walked with a sort of grim determination, knowing the odds said this was journey's end, the place he was moving toward for weeks, or maybe years—maybe all his life, and now he was there, here, the place, someplace, but not perhaps terribly well prepared, despite all that had passed recently, for the moment that would happen as soon as hundreds of feet dwindled to just a few.

The man finally looked his way, registered Grail, sized him up as though calculating the distance to him and definitely the distance away from him. Grail kept a steady pace and closed the gap, not wanting to appear hurried or to suggest danger. His father, after all, had become a willing exile. Then they were standing just four feet apart, each seeing just enough of themselves in the other's face to render introductions unnecessary, though it was Grail who finally offered to be redundant, "My father, I presume."

Grail said it in as detached a tone as he could muster, even thought fleetingly that it echoed "Dr. Livingston, I presume," which struck him as ludicrous and odd and silly—even though he had doctor in front of his name, too—but yet somehow it was also inevitable and very definitely appropriate.

Lewis Hudson regarded Grail coolly, but not with hostility. "If you're the famous Dr. Grail Hudson, then, yes, I'm Lewis Hudson, your father."

"I'm Grail. Just Grail." He belatedly offered his hand and Lewis accepted it in a brief, soft handshake.

Lewis smiled at his son. "But you are famous," he said. "I've read that book of yours. Interesting stuff. You don't care for us Southerners much."

"I suppose not," Grail said. "Maybe I can autograph a copy for you. To Dear Dad. Maybe over brunch at the local yacht club."

Lewis nodded his head. "That likely?"

"Not very," Grail said.

Lewis nodded some more. "Then you've come to be the angry and forgotten son—is that it?"

"I don't know," Grail said, realizing he really didn't.

"No, I don't imagine you do," Lewis said. "I don't know that I would either, in your shoes."

"What shoes am I in?" Grail said.

"Pretty muddy ones," Lewis said, offering a smile. Grail was tempted to return it, felt the corners of his mouth yearn to suddenly spring up, but he kept them at bay.

"There's not too damn much of this island that's dry," Grail said as he glanced at his boots.

"How did you find me?" Lewis said.

"Mom mentioned this place when I saw her last. It seemed the most likely choice for a man who needed a hiding place."

"And how is your mother—how is Lorraine?"

"Very well."

"She still teaching, in Michigan?"

"She still is. Kalamazoo."

"I see," Lewis said. "And how long have you known about me? Last I recall that was to be kept a secret."

"She told me a few weeks ago, when I was up there for a visit."

"Why did she do that?" Lewis rubbed his chin and then ran a hand through his bristly hair. "Only a few weeks, eh? Well, then you're boots are muddier than they look, aren't they."

"It would seem so," Grail said.

"Are you alone?"

As Grail replied he thought how funny it truly sounded: "Elvis is with me."

Lewis grinned and shook his head. "Elvis Presley. You two are like Batman and Robin."

That one made Grail smile, if ever so slightly and unwillingly.

"I saw you and Elvis, in Washington," Lewis said. "I suppose you know that, though."

"I was told, yes."

"Anybody else with you besides Elvis—anybody I should worry about?"

"Is there a reason for you to worry?"

"There might be," Lewis said. "Hell, there's always a reason to look over your shoulder, Mr. Professor."

"Grail. Just Grail."

"Ok, Grail."

"No, there's nobody except Robert. He's making a film on Elvis. I expected to find them on this side of the island. Maybe they got lost."

"Not enough of Bloodsworth to get lost in," Lewis said.

"You don't know Elvis, or Robert," Grail said.

"No, I don't. Not my world."

Grail turned toward the bay. "Just what *is* your world.?"

"Do you mean, am I a terrorist?"

"For starters, yeah," Grail said.

"No. I'm not. But you're going to have to take my word on that. I can't prove nothing, though there's not so damn much to be proved. It's complicated."

"No it isn't," Grail said. "Either you are or you aren't."

Lewis walked down to the water, his hands on his hips. He stared out at nothing in particular. Grail watched his back, felt—what did he feel? That was the maddening part: he wasn't sure. Some anxiety, some curiosity, and yes, definitely some anger. But was it worth the anger? He didn't know this man, his father. He wasn't sure what was to be gained from knowing him, though it was clear enough he had to come to this island and see for himself.

"I grew up with some people, some men, who could be extreme," Lewis said. "When I was younger, much younger, I thought I knew the world. Thought I knew it because I figured it was black and white. Not complicated. Us and them kind of stuff.

"Guilty by association?" Grail said.

"Something like that," Lewis said. "I belonged to a couple groups—folks they now call radicals. We opposed the union. Thought ourselves Confederates—Rebs. You know, like Jeb Stuart and Stonewall Jackson in the old days. Every time that reunification talk came up we opposed it. I worked for that group, got the word out. Door to door, even. Rallies. My politics went in the record, if you know what I mean. I was arrested once, at a rally that got out of hand. Some folks got hurt, but I swear all I did that day was try to get out, to run. Anyway, I was there. There's no denying it, and I got painted with the same brush as other fellows, the ones that would go too far sometimes. That sort of thing is always just behind you, in your wake. It don't go away."

"But that's all in the past now, right?" Grail said. "Now you're just misunderstood? Is that it? A victim of circumstances? And now we just close the door to the past and catch up, I suppose. You tell me what you've done the past 40 years, where you lived and all that. I tell you about my life, my house and garden, my job, the decent neighbors next door that sometimes offer a beer. You know, that getting to know you crap fathers and sons do at picnics and reunions."

"Being a professor sure has given you a quick tongue," Lewis said. "I suppose that's part of *your* world."

Grail stood next to him and looked out at the bay. The water was very calm, like glass. Grail took a long, slow breath and let it out slowly. He knew he had gotten too worked up. Calm was always more effective than anger when dealing with his students. He just had to remind himself and settle down. After all, what did he care? No, that was false. Be honest. He cared. He wouldn't be here if he didn't.

"OK," Grail said. "OK. Maybe we start small, and work up to the other stuff. One thing at a time, I guess."

"Maybe so," Lewis said. "I'm game."

"Where do you live?" Grail said. "I mean, where's home away from Bloodsworth Fucking Island?"

"Different places in Maryland," Lewis said. "Up by Frederick for a good long time. Now I live just over the sound, on the mainland."

"Do you work? How do you make a living?"

"I was a machinist," Lewis said. "I made all sorts of things, mostly in factories, but some years out of my own garage. I don't need so much to live."

"Did you like it?"

Lewis shrugged. "I didn't hate it. It was a living."

"And now?" Grail said.

"Now it's a retirement, a union pension. Funny, ain't it? A union man fighting the union."

"Is that one of the lessons you learned?" Grail said. "Irony."

Lewis faced him and studied his face. "Yeah, I learned irony, Mr. Professor. That probably shocks you, to hear I learned anything at all. Living to be old means eventually you learn something wasn't right when you was young. Sure, I learned that."

"Now you're just retired—other than being confused for a terrorist." Grail said. "That little misunderstanding."

"Before all this terrorist nonsense I did odd jobs to help pay bills. Right now I'm hiding out, but other than that I lead a pretty quiet life."

"More banter between father and son," Grail said.

"You just can't let it go, can you?" Lewis said. "What's your anger going to get you? The past has done happened. It happened so many years ago that me and your mom would be hard pressed to remember the facts accurate anymore. It just ended and that was that. She wanted me dead and buried so she told you whatever she told you, and I was—until now. Did you come to play catch or something?"

"There were others around when I was a kid to play catch with," Grail said. "My uncle."

"Well, that's ducky," Lewis said. "I'm glad George pitched in. Judging by it all, he didn't do a bad job. You made something of yourself. Hell, you're Elvis Presley's sidekick."

"Is that fatherly pride?"

"No, Grail, that's just one man telling another he's Ok."

"I suppose," Grail thought: Yes, I am OK. I know that. It's real enough. "Anyway, I don't think you have to hide anymore."

"Why is that?" Lewis was suspicious.

"I don't think anything will come of it," Grail said. "Elvis talked to the secret service types and they appear to be satisfied you aren't involved."

"Really?" Lewis said. "That's the gospel truth?" He had a look of genuine surprise, Grail thought, though the word "gospel" was irritating for a reason he could not quite put his finger on.

"Elvis seems to know these things," Grail said. "It's one of his gifts."

Lewis frowned. "Maybe so. But there'll have to be a conversation. They won't just let it sweep by. Some suits will show up, if even to just roust me some. They'll want to let me know they're around."

"I don't know about that," Grail said. "Maybe that's so." He studied his father's face but really could not discern his emotions at that moment. "But they didn't seem to know where you are."

"Did you tell them?"

"No. I've never talked to them about you. I can't speak for Elvis, but my guess is he didn't tell them where we we're going. Or maybe he told them about the documentary Robert is making, how we we're going to drive around and film at a bunch of locations."

"You were probably followed."

"Well, I didn't notice anyone," Grail said.

"Doesn't matter," Lewis said. "It'll play out the way it's supposed to."

"You're a fatalist," Grail said.

"A realist," Lewis said. "How about you?"

"I think I've become a realist, too," Grail said, not all sure that he was. More awkward silence settled between them like fog. A couple of times they looked at each other, neither willing to make the glance last more than a moment.

"Where do you go from here?" Grail said. "Will you go back to the mainland? Do you want a ride back? How did—I mean, I don't even know how you got here. I know you probably didn't swim."

"That's quite a swim," Lewis said. "I have a small boat up aways. It's tucked under some trees. But thanks for the offer. I'll go back in a few days."

"What's there to stay here for exactly?"

Lewis smiled. "Not very much, but it's been a while since I was here. This was the place that grabbed my imagination when I was a kid. It was like visiting an island pirates could use. It was like being a pirate. It's just memories now, but I'll stay on a day or two until the food situation gets dicey—until I get tired of Spam and canned chili. I can fish, and think some. Solitude is a good thing from time to time. Don't get me wrong—I'm no hermit. But this is a good place to think."

"Too spare for me," Grail said, looking down the lonely stretch of beach. "But I think I'm glad I saw it."

"Really? Why are you glad, Grail?"

Grail thought about it, creating a long and uneasy silence. He felt his father's eyes again scanning his face, and for the first time since they met he felt the cold stab of fear that comes from not knowing what to do next. "I don't know. I guess

I'm learning there are plenty of things that mostly can just be felt, but not said very well."

"Yes," Lewis said. "There's plenty of that."

"And there are things that take time before you know what they mean," Grail added.

"The world isn't black and white, is it," Lewis said. "That's my great discovery. It just took a long damn time to get past black and white."

"Blue and gray," Grail muttered, a smile forming slowly on his face.

"What's that?"

"Nothing. A stray bolt of irony."

"You're the professor," Lewis said.

And the father, too, Grail thought, and it was finally not a surprise but a confirmation. A man ultimately is his own father because he keeps growing, if he's lucky, and as he grows he's the only person there every damn day to help get past the rough spots. We become our own fathers, and we should, and we must raise ourselves, even when a biological father has been there, but even more so when one has not. In the end we are solitary creatures. We're alone. The smart ones will make alliances and coalitions with others to make the trip sweeter and kinder, but it's a long and solitary trip and in the end the partners we make can't get us across the last barrier. That we have to do for ourselves.

What barrier? Grail knew there was one. He felt it. God? Afterlife? Death? Somehow he understood—in that way of knowing without being able to say it—that all those elements were ingredients of the barrier, that it was a mystery, sure, but perhaps a sweet one in the end. What Grail really knew, better and clearer than anything else, was that right then he had taken it as far as he could understand. The rest would have to come on another day. On a series of many days, stretching over the remaining course of his life. Right up to the bridge spanning the barrier.

"Time for me to shove off, then," Grail said. "Elvis shouldn't be left on his own too long. Lord knows what can happen."

"Is he crazy?" Lewis said.

Grail laughed. "No. He's one of the sanest people I've ever met."

Lewis offered his hand and this time they shook with some feeling.

"Until next time," Grail said.

"Next time," Lewis said. "You take care of yourself, Grail. But I can see you've done a good job of taking care."

Grail was tempted to say something, but he knew it wouldn't be helpful, would be irrelevant, really. He didn't need Lewis Hudson. And the time for guilt and blame had passed. It had passed easier than he expected and for that he was grateful. He walked away, feeling his father's eyes on his back. After a few seconds he turned and saw his father wave.

"*Is* there a next time?" Grail called.

"You know where to find me," Lewis said. "And I know where to find you."

"Absolutely," Grail said. He threw his father a salute and then turned and headed toward the tree line. He glanced up once, at a flock of geese in tight formation. Their honking was faint, but Grail could hear it. He watched as the lead goose relinquished his spot and another slid into its place.

978-0-595-67385-8
0-595-67385-6

Printed in the United Kingdom
by Lightning Source UK Ltd.
107287UKS00002B/15